An Excerpt fro

Lost Romance Ranch

Wendie looked in his kind, tired eyes, and suddenly her heart filled. She swallowed back a moment of shame for letting her own fear and hardness keep her from realizing that she hadn't given Teague a real second chance, this man she'd vowed to love and honor for all her life. She could not go forward with anything as destructive as breaking up a family without giving their marriage every opportunity to survive. She'd keep her guard up, but she had to open her mind and heart to all possibilities. She had to open her mind, heart, and home.

"I will probably regret this before your stay is over, and I don't want you reading too much into it, but..." She stole a peek over her shoulder at the place she had meant as her haven from the influence of this very man, then sighed.

"Are you suggesting I stay with you?" The old energy infused his tone again.

She tugged her robe closed all the way to the neck. "The couch in the living room pulls out into a bed."

"Fine. Good. Thanks."

She pivoted on her heel and hurried back across the lawn, calling after her, "You can park in the extra slot for my apartment; it's marked in the lot. If you need anything, look around. Don't bother trying to ask me where to find it."

"Why not?"

She turned and gave him one last look. "Because I'll be in my room, banging my head against the locked door for being such a soft touch."

She wasn't sure because her heartbeat was pounding so loudly in her ears, but she thought she heard him answer, "You won't regret this, Wendie. I promise."

As she slipped through her front door, she murmured a silent prayer that her husband was right and asked the Lord to guide her decisions about this, as she no longer trusted her own judgment.

Our **Giggle** Guarantee

We're so sure our books will make you smile, giggle, or laugh out loud that we're putting our "giggle guarantee" behind each one. If this book fails to tickle your funny bone, return it to your local bookstore and exchange it for another in our romantic comedy line.

Lost Romance Ranch

ANNIE JONES

WATERBROOK
PRESS

LOST ROMANCE RANCH
PUBLISHED BY WATERBROOK PRESS
5446 North Academy Boulevard, Suite 200
Colorado Springs, Colorado 80918
A division of Random House, Inc.

ISBN 1-57856-135-3

Library of Congress Cataloging-in-Publication Data
Jones, Annie, 1957-
Lost Romance Ranch / Annie Jones. — 1st ed.
p. cm. — (Route 66 romantic comedy series ; bk. 3)
ISBN 1-57856-135-3
1. United States Highway 66—Fiction. 2. Automobile travel—Fiction. 3. Separated people—Fiction. I. Title. II. Series.

PS3560.O45744 L67 2000
813'.54—dc21 00-022410

Printed in the United States of America
2000—First Edition

10 9 8 7 6 5 4 3 2 1

Prologue

Hay crunched under Wendie's boots. The May breeze carried the sweet smells of spring in California, the promise of good things to come. Wendie felt no such promise in her heart.

She clucked her tongue softly as she led her horse to his rented stall after a long, thoughtful ride. Riding had always meant a great deal to her. She'd first found her love and talent for it and for working with horses as a child actress on a long-running show, *The Lost Romance Ranch*. There she had found the three things that had shaped and given meaning to her life ever since: her faith in God, her gift for working with horses, and the man she loved and later married.

Wendie sighed. She had hoped the time spent at the stable would clear her head and lift the heaviness in her heart. It usually did.

She had nowhere else to go, no person to talk to about her anxieties and the options left open to her. She had turned her troubles over to the Lord and prayed until she no longer knew how to pray. As comforting as prayer was, she longed for someone to sit down and hear her out.

But who? This was not the kind of thing she could

ever burden her twelve-year-old twins with. And she couldn't talk to her husband. Heaven knows she'd tried that until she was bone weary from the effort. He never seemed to hear a word she said or understand her thoughts and feelings about life, their marriage, and what it took to build a strong family.

"That's the whole problem in a nutshell, isn't it, Roanie?" She patted her gentle horse on the neck. "Teague Blackwell."

Roanie snorted.

"You can say that again." She guided the animal into the narrow stall and began to work the saddle's cinch loose. "Sometimes I think you listen to me better than my own husband. When he's even around to listen."

As she pulled the saddle off and went about putting the horse's gear away, she tried not to dwell on the events of the previous night. But the images kept creeping into her thoughts of the kids' sixth-grade "graduation" celebration. The sparkling house, the homemade cake, the excited and hopeful faces of her children filled her mind. All followed by the haunting reality of the empty chair where her husband should have been sitting with them gathered around the dining room table.

"It was for a good cause," Teague later insisted. And, "They're homeschooled, Wendie. We can easily reschedule our end-of-the-school-year party for another time."

He was right on both counts, which only made her more angry. She was painfully aware of Teague's priorities: a tireless work ethic, a need to give to those less fortunate, and a desire to provide for his family's future. However, she and the children always found themselves far down that list of laudable priorities. When it came to his time and attention, his loved ones got short shrift, even if what he was doing was for their own benefit.

Last night Teague had proven that once again. He had stayed later than expected at a board meeting for Christian Children's International Charities, the organization for which he was a spokesman. How hurt and disappointed the twins were, and how bravely they tried to hide it. But they couldn't hide it from her, and their father had dragged in too late for him to even tell them good night.

When he finally came home after they'd all given up and gone to bed, Teague had awakened her to "big news." He'd signed a contract for three months' worth of work on a soap opera! Signed the deal without so much as talking it over with Wendie first. This commitment of time and energy would take up most of the twins' summer vacation.

"I had plans for this summer, Roanie." She began to groom the horse, brushing his thick mane with long, easy strokes. "Big plans of my own. Teague knew that. Or at least he should have known that if he was listening to me when I told him about Texas and the ranch and my hopes and dreams."

She thought of the small town in Texas where she'd hoped they'd spend their summer. She thought of the Flying C Dude Ranch, where the kids were booked for a week of summer camp in August. She grieved for the time she had hoped she and Teague would spend there, lost to them now. "I was even hoping…now this may sound silly, but I was hoping to bring you out there, Roanie."

The gentle red quarter horse pawed at the ground.

"You see, I thought…" She smoothed her hand down

the animal's broad rib cage. "I thought maybe, if we were out there, away from all the things that put demands on Teague, that he might see we could have a different way of life."

Roanie's tail swished to flick a fly off his flank.

"Not that he'd have to give up acting, mind you. He just doesn't get that many offers anymore that he couldn't live somewhere else and still work as much as he does now." She clenched the brush tighter in her hand. The horse shied away from her, kicking up bits of hay and dust. They glimmered in a beam of brilliant California sunshine.

"Sorry, boy. Thinking about that soap-opera deal made me brush a bit harder than I meant to." She smoothed her palm over Roanie's sleek shoulder. "It's not like we need the money, you know. Especially if we'd invest what we have in something else that can help to support and provide for us...like a certain dude ranch I hear might be up for sale soon. You'd like that, wouldn't you, big guy? Living in Texas, having a place to gallop and go for long rides with other horses? Having a life where home and family came first?"

The horse nickered.

"I know I'd like it. And the kids would too. The kids need it." She bit her lower lip. "Maybe it's time those things became priorities for me, even if they never will be for Teague."

Her stomach lurched. She could hardly swallow for the lump wedged high in her throat. She'd been thinking about this for a long time now. That did not make her decision any easier.

But Teague's casual treatment of the family occasion and his surprise announcement had been the last straw. She had to do something. She had to do what was best for herself and her children. If her actions startled Teague into realizing how much was at stake and the necessity for him to change his ways, then she'd be forever grateful. If not…

She shut her eyes and laid her cheek against Roanie's neck.

If not, then she would do whatever it took to give her children the best life possible—even if she had to do it without Teague.

Dear Teague,

You have no idea how hard it is for me to write this letter.

No harder than it was for him to read it. Surely not. At least, in writing the note that told him she'd taken their children and left him, Wendie had known what was coming. Teague had not.

How could he have known? Troubles in the marriage, sure, he'd admit to those, even to his part in them. But had things really gotten so bad that Wendie felt she had no alternatives left but to leave him?

He slumped into a chair at the kitchen table, the letter he'd found propped up there in his hand. He tried to read the words again, but his eyes would not focus. He tried to understand what had just happened to his life, but his mind would not comprehend.

The silence in the house enveloped him. Beyond the

halo of light around the small table, there were only darkened rooms. If he had wrapped up his last-minute meeting with his agent faster, he might have come home in time to catch them still here. He felt numb.

This could not be happening. He had worked so hard and so long doing all the right things. He had been a good father and a good provider in a line of work where longevity and prosperity only came to a select few. He had worked and scraped and saved and given his family everything they could want or need. He looked at the letter in his hand. Apparently that was not enough.

He smoothed the single page of stationery on the table and folded his hands on top of it. "Please, Lord, show me what to do. My heart says I should go after her, but I have to report to the set tomorrow. There is no way I can go looking for her in Texas and be at work in the morning."

He glanced up at the clock. Almost midnight. According to the note, she'd left six hours earlier. She could be anywhere along the road, probably tucked in some motel. He'd never guess which one or in what town.

Once I get settled, I will let you know how you can reach me. The letter crinkled beneath his hand. Maybe he could go out as soon as he heard from her…and do what? She made it clear she wanted his full attention; going out for a day or a weekend would surely do more harm than good. Nothing short of walking away from his new job would allow him to work on this rift with the right kind of commitment.

"I can't do it, Lord. I can't violate the contract I just signed. People are depending on me here. My family, even in another state—even more so in another state, running two households—is relying on my financial support. I have two children who need to know that their father is a man whose word is his bond. I represent a charity that needs a spokesman who isn't considered a flake for running out on his obligations. And I have a wife who wants me to devote my time to her. How can I do all that, Lord?"

There had to be a way.

Teague had to find a way to fix this. Even if he could not do it immediately, he would do it. With God's help, hard work, and a little ingenuity, he'd find a way to keep providing for his family's future, to spend as much time as possible with Wendie, and to win his wife and kids back.

One

A brown panel truck lumbered to a halt outside Wendie Blackwell's new residence. The delivery, she told herself, could be for any one of her neighbors in the small apartment complex where she and the twins had moved three months ago. But the delivery would not be for a neighbor, and she knew it. The oversize white pouch in the truck driver's hands was for her.

She stole a peek out her first-floor window. The man checked his clipboard, squinted at the building, then headed up the walk. In his shorts and ball cap, the ideal uniform for the hot August afternoon in Texas, he headed her way with a loping gait. He hardly seemed threatening.

Yet Wendie's pulse picked up. She twisted a lock of hair around her finger. She ducked away from the window and pressed her back to the door.

She thought for an instant of staying right there and not answering the bell she knew would ring at any moment. But she'd have to answer it. Otherwise the man would only return tomorrow or, worse yet, leave the loathsome parcel with a neighbor. She couldn't have that.

No one in the tiny town of Castle Mesa, Texas, the place she had so carefully chosen as the perfect refuge from her former life, would understand. No one would keep her closely guarded secret. Wouldn't her story make great gossip down at the beauty parlor? Or the perfect complement to a large order of fries and gravy at the Double Heart Diner out on what was once Route 66? And how tongues might wag out at the Flying C Dude Ranch if they ever made the connection!

She could not let that happen. Swallowing hard, she swung the door open before the delivery man had the chance to so much as knock.

"Got another one for you, ma'am." He grinned and thrust the package toward her, quickly followed by his trusty clipboard. "Guess you know the drill by now."

She tried to smile. "Uh-huh."

"You've had a delivery every day for a solid week now, haven't you?"

"Has it really been that long?" It felt so much longer.

"Sign on the bottom line please."

Wendie scribbled her legal name, Gwendalyn Blackwell, while hugging the package to her chest, then thanked the man.

He put his fingers to the tip of his hat and nodded good-bye. "I'd say I'll see you tomorrow, but we don't deliver on weekends."

His words brought an odd sense of relief to Wendie as she shut the door. She examined the container for any hints as to who might have sent it. No delivery tomorrow, and no indication of the sender. The two realizations canceled each other out, leaving her feeling nothing in particular but tired. This game was wearing her down.

That in itself made her think of one person. But, she

had argued with herself, he wouldn't torment her like this. Would he? Maybe this time the gift would carry more of a clue.

She ripped away the wide, clear tape sealing the plastic pouch, then peered inside. Her stomach knotted. Her hands trembled a bit, not from fear but from a potent mix of emotions that ranged from anger to agony—yes, and a little bit of fear. She tipped up the pouch.

A long, slender rope slithered from the opening and fell into a neat coil at her feet. She stepped back and with that movement must have jarred the package enough to send a slip of paper somersaulting to the floor. She rubbed her thumb and forefinger together, unsure if she really wanted to pick the thing up. Then she sighed and grabbed it.

Eleven-thirty, your time, on local channel three. Don't you dare miss it.

She turned the paper over, but there was only this short typewritten note. Or would it better be described as a threat?

"Whatcha got there, Mom?"

"Did you get another mysterious package from the past?"

Wendie jerked her head up. Immediately she found her suspicions about who could be behind the gifts reinforced by the deep green of her children's eyes. They were so like their father, these two, from the tops of their black-haired heads to the tips of their sassy tongues. That fact warmed Wendie's heart—and broke it—nearly every day.

She forced a grin and tucked the note into her pocket, giving her son and daughter all the assurance she had to spare. "It's nothing for you to worry about. Let's get dinner started, and you can tell me about your day."

The rest of the evening passed in agonizing slow motion. Even so, Wendie found herself dawdling to draw out the last few moments of the day with her children.

"Mom, I'm twelve. I don't need tucking in," Sean told her in a voice that sometimes cracked into a deeper tone.

"So humor me. Just let me stand here in the doorway and blow you a good-night kiss."

He grumbled something in reply. She kissed her hand and blew the invisible symbol of her affection.

"You can kiss me good-night, Mom." Kate called from the next bedroom. "I'll humor you."

"Thanks." She went into the room, smoothed her hand over the hot pink-and-orange bedspread, and kissed her daughter on the cheek. "Knowing what you're willing to go through for your silly old mother means a lot."

"Oh, Mom, no one thinks you're silly."

The child had intended it as a compliment. Still, Wendie couldn't help but feel a twinge of disappointment that the girl hadn't said, "No one thinks you're old."

"Sleep tight," she whispered to her daughter. "Don't forget to say your prayers."

"I won't." Kate nodded, ever serious; then, just as Wendie reached the doorway and flipped off the light, Kate admonished, "You, too."

In the hallway outside their rooms, Wendie did linger to say a fervent prayer. Whatever this latest note and string of gifts meant, she prayed it would not jeopardize the tenuous new life she had begun for her children's sake.

That done, she crept into the living room. She opened the doors of the cabinet where their TV remained unused most of the time. She had never regretted her decision to put strict limits on the viewing habits of her family. She would often lecture her would-be prime-time junkies on the perils of watching too much mindless entertainment.

Still, sometimes television could enlighten and educate. She hoped this proved just such a time. She settled onto the couch with a soda and some popcorn waiting on the table nearby and curled her legs beneath her. She wet her lips and pressed the button on the remote. The set popped and crackled and came to life just as the familiar late-night talk-show music began to play.

Gamely, she sat through the monologue. She yawned over a cornball comedy sketch and tried to stay focused on a halfhearted movie pitch by the hottest actress of the minute. Try as she might, she could not find any connection between anything she saw here and the gifts she'd received all week long.

She thought for a moment of the packages now stuffed in the back of her closet. A reproduction of a vintage road map. A white cowboy hat. A gold pin in the shape of a tiny pair of angel's wings and a rope, a snippet of a western lariat, to be precise. She could hardly make a case to connect them to each other, much less to what she saw on the talk show. Except that she recognized every object as a memento from her own past, from the television show that had played such a big role in her life.

The show and its memories that she was trying so hard now to escape.

She turned her attention to the screen again. When someone from the San Diego Zoo appeared next with some exotic animals, Wendie considered giving up and just switching the program off. She lifted the remote and aimed it, her finger over the power button. But as they cut away to the commercial break, the teaser for the next guest made her freeze.

"Stay with us because you won't want to miss tonight's final guest. You'll remember him best for his nine-year stint as Ryder on the popular TV show of the seventies and eighties *The Lost Romance Ranch.* We'll be right back."

The screen filled with a blaring advertisement for something they claimed everyone had to have. Wendie did not know what, nor did she care. Her heart hammered in her ears and her throat had gone dry. Voicelessly, she mouthed the name that had been on her mind, the one person she had not wanted to believe was behind the weeklong parade of stress and unwelcome emotions, Teague Blackwell.

She blinked. She tried to catch her breath. Seeing Teague on television wasn't so strange, she told herself. That was his element. Fame and celebrity were like a lifeline to the man. So much so that when she had finally had enough of his drive and ambition coming before everything and moved to rural Texas, he had chosen to remain in California.

Wendie gritted her teeth. She wanted to flick the show off and storm upstairs, but as the words of the note had forewarned, she did not dare. She had to stay put and see what Teague had up his sleeve so she could find a way to defend her heart and her children against it.

"Welcome, everybody, if you would, please, Teague Blackwell." The host's words snapped her attention back to the program.

The audience cheered, and the theme music to the hit show that was Teague's crowning glory reached a crescendo. The curtains fluttered.

Wendie bit her lip.

Teague stepped from backstage, his hand raised and his smile on high beam.

It had only been three months since she'd seen him last. Yet, when he finished the expected greetings and dropped into the chair, and the camera came in for a closeup, it felt like a lifetime since Wendie had looked into those eyes.

She held her breath. She closed her hand around her half-empty soda can. She tried to look away, but she simply could not do it. *Teague.*

Though he looked every bit of his thirty-nine years, Wendie still saw in him the young man who had first won her heart. His jet-black hair, with silver now starting to show at the temples, looked as thick and in the same charming state of disarray as always. He was still lean, though broader across the shoulders, his chest filled out as it had not been in his youth. The hint of laugh lines framed his smile and crinkled out from the corners of his deep-set eyes. She exhaled a slow, shaky breath. Even though miles, time zones, and heartaches separated them, Wendie could feel the focus of his sparkling eyes.

How could he still have that staggering effect on her,

after all the pain he had put her through? She wished she knew. Then maybe she would know how to steel herself against it.

"You are a hot property these days, Teague." The host spoke as if they were the best of pals. "But then being hot is something you're used to, huh? From the days when you made those teen magazine covers. And now you've been nominated by a fan digest as daytime television's hottest veteran hunk."

"Veteran hunk?" Teague gave a modest laugh. "Isn't that code for 'guy we'd most like to see in a denture commercial'?"

"I think it means you're a survivor of the great hunk wars—you all remember those, right?"

"Well, I am a survivor all right. But I don't get that whole hunk thing. That's not me." Teague shook his head and laughed again.

"Oh, sure it's not," Wendie muttered. "You're adorable, and you know it."

In truth, she knew he didn't see how irresistible many women found him. That added to his appeal. Despite his success, Teague remained a humble, kind, and decent human being.

Who loved acting more than he loved his own family. For one second, she contemplated throwing her soda can at the television.

"Not many child stars make it to adult acting careers, and for a while it looked like you'd be one of the ones showing up on the where-are-they-now lists."

"Better those than the when-do-they-make-parole list," Teague joked.

"That's true." The host chuckled. "But I have to ask you, to what do you attribute this latest comeback and newfound success?"

Success. That one word justified the whole outlay of time, money, and creativity behind the series of gifts Teague had sent to her home. They had insured that she would tune in and hear that one word, that one accolade.

"Actually, I wouldn't exactly call this a comeback, you know. That implies I've been out of the business." Teague flexed his large hands on the arms of the chair like a lion preparing to pounce. "I haven't been resting on my residuals all these years, you know. I've done Broadway and regional theater, taught acting, made the rounds of the old TV buff conferences, and even had a couple of albums that did all right."

"And add to that your current role of soap-opera heartthrob Dash Logan," the host played along congenially. "Now, I heard a rumor that you might be leaving the show. Is there any truth to it?"

An audible groan rose from the audience.

Wendie sat up.

"Yes, I'm afraid it's true. Ol' Dash Logan is heading off into daytime TV oblivion. That hunk is sunk."

She leaned forward.

"Sounds like you've got some disappointed fans." The host motioned toward the unseen audience.

"Well, I think we all saw it coming." Teague shifted in his seat, his expression sober but with a glint of mischief in his eyes. "Dash has been getting deeper and deeper into trouble for the last few weeks, what with his phony marriage to an unstable amnesiac starting to take on real romantic undertones, which would complicate his plans of murder to collect the insurance. Of course, it doesn't help that he already has a real wife, one he thinks died eight years ago but who in fact works at the same hospital where he is a doctor. You know that can't be good."

"When oh when are these daytime shows going to get off this reality kick and start doing stories that aren't carbon copies of the average person's life?" The host sat back with a sigh to overplay the wisecrack.

Teague laughed. "Pitiful, isn't it? Not like the good ol' days of television when moms did housework in heels and pearls, and kids were always cute as a button. Or when cowboys struggling to keep a Texas guest ranch in the black lived in a mansion, dressed like movie stars, and had a James Dean wannabe angel of Route 66 watching over them, huh?"

"*The Lost Romance Ranch.* That show's been off the air, what? A decade?"

"That's right, but it still runs in syndication around the world and has an active fan base, fueled by a crossover crowd of Route 66 enthusiasts."

"*Route 66?* I thought that was a different TV show."

"Well, it was a big road." Teague smiled and managed to sneak a wink into the camera.

Though she had not wanted to, Wendie returned the smile. She couldn't help it. Seeing her husband like this, hearing the quiet affection in his voice for the old show, still touched her.

"Truth is, *The Lost Romance Ranch* was intended to be one of those glamour shows, sort of *Dallas* meets *Hotel,* but it really didn't find its identity until it made the Route

66 connection. They brought in the mysterious character of Ryder, a loner who roamed the back roads of old Route 66. Then it became more of a human interest or issue show like *Highway to Heaven,* less about power and money."

"If I recall, they really narrowed down the cast then, and you became, for all intents and purposes, the star of the show at a very young age."

"I was a principal character, yes, but so many people went into making that an outstanding program."

Wendie bit her lip. Gorgeous, humble, generous to others. During this recent struggle in their marriage she'd forgotten those wonderful traits in the man she had married for better or worse.

"Remind me now, you played a ghost? Or some kind of angel?"

"They kept that ambiguous for the first few years. Eventually, the writers gave it an angelic twist, mostly because they wanted to throw in a hook that was based more on a storybook than the Good Book."

"Oh?"

"I became an angel-type figure hoping to earn a chance at becoming human instead of the ghost of a drifter haunting old Route 66, where the ranch was located."

"Now the Route 66 thing, I remember reading that the show's creator threw that in as an afterthought, sort of as an homage to the old road he loved in childhood. That highway was gone even back then, right?"

"Decommissioned about the same time the show really got going. But not gone. People remember it, what it stood for. They long for that, I think, the return to simplicity, the idea of a road that can take you someplace better, of people who are basically good-hearted and helpful."

Wendie put her hand to her throat, feeling as if his gaze had found her in the darkness of her quiet Texas apartment.

"People still want to make a connection with the past," he seemed to say directly to her. "They want to have hope for the future."

Wendie sniffed, defying the tears that were bathing her eyes. He was talking about television viewers, she told herself, not them, not their marriage and his hopes for reconciliation.

The host tapped his pencil on the desk. "They say there are folks who still think that the ranch really exists somewhere in Texas. People have been known to knock on doors asking for directions to it."

Teague smiled. "It's gratifying to think we created something people wanted so much they'd go looking for it. They obviously still want it."

"You'd better hope they still want it, right? Plans are in the works for a reunion movie."

"Actually, that's why I'm here. We've got a rough draft of a script, and we've got a green light, but one essential thing is missing."

A knot began to coil in the pit of Wendie's stomach. She put her soda aside and scooted to the very edge of her chair.

"We can't do a reunion show without one very important member of the cast."

She felt her lips form the word "no," but she said nothing.

"The only other primary character that was with the show from beginning to end…"

She ground her teeth together, her fingers gripping the upholstery, and waited like someone braced for an impact.

"Wendie, if you're watching this tonight, and I believe you are, what do you think?"

"What do I *think?*" She snatched up the remote and clicked the set off with vehemence. Tossing the changer aside, she sighed, then spoke aloud to the blank screen to chase away the taunting silence of the darkened room. "I think I am a complete idiot for letting my guard down for one moment where you're concerned, Teague Blackwell. You never put my feelings ahead of your own ambition. And I see now you never will."

Two

Have you gone completely nuts, Teague?" Wendie moved to shut the door right in his face. "A reunion show? You don't really think you can pull that off, do you?"

"Not without my costar, I can't. I need Claire, Wendie, and that's you." Teague stepped into the diminishing doorway, leading with a bouquet of a dozen red roses wrapped in green tissue paper.

His timing was off. The door fell shut, neatly decapitating about half of the elegant flowers.

"I meant to do a reunion of *The Lost Romance Ranch,* Wendie, not *The Addams Family.*"

The door jerked open.

He'd gotten her attention. He started forward.

A fistful of bruised scarlet petals came flying out into his face, smothering him with their sweet, pungent aroma. The door slammed shut again, this time followed by the solid clunk of a deadbolt sliding into place. Locked out. Wendie had locked him out without even listening to his idea, or bothering to find out why he had suggested the movie.

Teague put his hand on the paper card in a small brass

frame on the door. In Wendie's neat handwriting it read *The Blackwells.* He sighed. Not all the Blackwells lived here. One Blackwell, the original owner of the name, lived in a small southwestern-style house in a quiet part of Los Angeles. He had no key to let himself into his family's home and no words to let himself into his wife's heart.

Wendie was his wife; she always would be. So what if she had gathered the twins and moved halfway across the country three months ago saying they were through? Teague could not accept that. Neither did Wendie. He saw it flickering in her eyes when she first opened her door and found him waiting on the other side.

Things had never gone smoothly for the two of them, but they always had each other, so it didn't matter. As long as the problems came from the outside, they could handle anything with faith, love, and hard work. But when their relationship began to fall apart...

And Teague had not helped things. He understood that now, though he still felt hard-pressed to see how he had gone wrong, why Wendie had suddenly wanted to turn her back on the life they had built. It seemed that in the last year or so, she had concentrated on all the bad things their unusual life-style had given them. None of the good.

Had she forgotten the way they'd reached out to people everywhere? The money they'd raised for charity? The Bible study they'd started for struggling actors? Or the wonderful adventures they'd had along the way? How much they had laughed? How much they had loved each other?

He wanted to show her those things again, and she

wanted more time with him. They both needed to go back to the way things used to be. The reunion movie was, to him, the perfect way to accomplish it all.

Why wouldn't she even give him the chance to talk to her about this? He stood back from the door. August in Texas was pretty hot. Maybe she had a window open or at least unlocked somewhere in her ground-floor apartment. If he could just get in…

He glanced down at the crumpled roses in his hand and winced. It didn't take much imagination to guess what might happen to him if he stuck his head in one of Wendie's windows. He rubbed his hand over the back of his neck. Still, he had to see Wendie and his children. He would not leave until he found a way.

"Psst."

Teague jerked his head up and looked around but saw nothing.

"Psst."

He whipped his entire body around. The roses in his hand smacked into the doorframe, mangling the few remaining flowers midstem so that they bowed down like limp rag dolls. "Is somebody out there, or does this building have a slow leak?"

"Dad? *Psst.* Dad! Over here!"

He caught a glimpse of his daughter Katie's dark hair as she darted around the edge of the building.

It warmed his heart to see his child again. He hurried toward her. In a matter of seconds, he'd rounded the building and run head-on into Katie's open arms.

"Hi, sweetie, it's so good to see you." He wrapped her in a tight hug. "I've missed you so much."

"Hey, what about me?" Sean crossed his arms over his narrow chest.

"I've missed you, too, Son." Teague reached out and tousled the boy's damp hair. "Especially when my grass needed cutting and I had to break down and do it myself."

"Ha, you would break down if you had to mow your own grass. You Hollywood types are helpless about that kind of thing," Sean teased, exaggerating a newly acquired Texas accent.

Teague laughed. "Yeah, you know us Hollywood types, we can't meet a total stranger on the street without giving them a big old hug and kiss, either."

He left the rose bouquet with Katie and lurched toward his son, making smooching sounds that sent his daughter giggling and his son groaning as if he had a three-day bellyache. When Teague caught Sean, he gave him a sincere hug, then put his arm around the boy's shoulders.

Despite the heat, Teague felt a chill. He looked down. A big wet spot stretched from the middle of his chest to his knees. He gave his kids a more thorough once-over and realized that beneath their oversize T-shirts, they wore sopping-wet swimming suits. "What are you two doing out here?"

"We were down by the apartment pool." Sean jerked his thumb over his shoulder.

"Yeah, thanks for warning me about that before I hugged you both."

They laughed as he pinched at his soaked T-shirt, shook his leg, then pounded the heel of his hand against the side of his head as if he'd even gotten water in his ear.

Then Katie grew serious. "We were on our way back to the apartment when we heard you and Mom fighting."

"We weren't fighting." Technically that wasn't a lie. Their encounter had been so brief they hadn't had a chance to fight.

"What would you call it then?" Sean cocked his head, his eyes narrowed. "Rehearsal for that reunion movie you want to do?"

"You know about that?"

"Not only do we know about it, Dad, we're all for it!" The twins both began to chatter about the idea at the same time.

Teague didn't even bother to try to decipher the babble. He just allowed himself to revel in the presence of his two greatest fans. They had so much of their mother in them. Not so much in their physical attributes as in their gentle spirits, their caring attitudes, their enthusiasm for life, and their love for him. In those ways they were pure Wendie.

Wendie still loved him. That could not have changed. That and his big plans for their future gave him hope.

"Don't worry, Dad. We have a key. You can be our guest." Katie dangled a lone key on a rainbow key chain before him.

"Thank you, kitten, but I think I'd better wait for your mother's invitation. It's her home."

"It's our home too," Katie whispered.

"It should be your home, Dad." Sean set his jaw.

They stood there a moment in silence, none of them seeming to know what to say or do until Sean spoke up. "Of course, if you're set on waiting for Mom to ask you in, maybe you should go back to California. You'll know real easy when her invitation is coming. Just watch for a delivery from a flying pig!"

Teague chuckled. "Maybe we won't have to wait that long, Son."

"Wish we could help." Katie chewed at her lower lip.

"Maybe you can. If you think you're up to a little playacting?" He raised an eyebrow at them.

They assured him they were.

"Okay, then here's what I want you to do..."

Three minutes later, Teague got his invitation.

"Teague Blackwell, get yourself in here right now!"

Wendie stood in the open doorway and squinted into the glaring afternoon sun. The sight of Teague warmed her more than she had expected. Though that set off warning flares inside her brain, she struggled to keep her breathing steady and her features indifferent. She didn't want him to see how much his nearness affected her.

"Ah, Wendie! It's so good to see you."

"You're not staying. We're just going to get this little incident with the twins worked out, and then you will be on your way. Got it?"

"You look terrific." He pulled a bent and bedraggled bouquet from behind his back and offered it to her.

She did not take the flowers but gave him a slow, deliberate once-over instead. "You look a mess."

He swiped his hand down his wet shirt.

"Guess the kids got carried away when they hugged me. It's been so long since we've seen each other..."

Guilt. She should have known he'd stoop to yet another trick to try to wheedle his way under her skin. Well, it wasn't going to work.

"I can't tell you how good it felt to hug those guys again. It's something I've dreamed of for..." His gaze darted away. "It was worth getting soaked to the skin."

Okay, so guilt worked on her. Why should she be any different than most people? She snatched the pathetic roses from his hand. "Come in. I'll get you a towel."

She did not look back to see if he walked inside or what kind of reaction he might have to seeing her new home for the first time. She headed straight for the kitchen, laid the sorry bouquet in the sink, then grabbed a fluffy towel that she'd had handy to mop up after the kids if they dripped water in after their swim. Calm, cool, above it all—that's how she would act.

Taking a deep breath, she shook back her hair, turned on her heel, and let out a sharp, breathy gasp.

Teague stepped back, putting a whole two feet of distance between them.

She slapped lightly at his arm. "Don't sneak up on me like that! I thought you were in the living room."

"Sorry. I followed you right on in because I thought—"

"Because you thought you own the place, just like you own any space you're in. Well, not *this* space, buddy."

"Wendie, I—"

She waved her hand to cut him off. "This is the one little piece of the world where your bigger-than-life personality does not get you carte blanche to go and do whatever you please."

"I never—"

"This is my home, okay? You can't come in and just take charge of everything, you got that?"

"I just wanted to dry off."

"What?" She blinked.

He spread his hands to show the dark spots on his shirt and jeans.

"Oh. Yeah. I knew that." She thrust the towel at him. "Here."

He patted the towel over the water stains. "Just a tiny bit defensive, huh?"

"I have a right to be after you used the kids to get yourself into my home. Threatening to see if the local newspaper wanted to do a piece on your visit? That was low."

"I didn't threaten anything. I told the kids the truth—that I planned to do whatever it took to get your attention, to get you to talk to me." He grinned. "Desperate times call for desperate measures."

Nobody but Teague could have made that cornball line sound positively sincere, even touching. If she didn't know what an excellent actor the man could be, she might have leaned toward forgiving him, at least for this antic.

"You have to know that I would never use the kids to hurt you in any way. If I thought you'd have taken it as anything but a joke, a goofy backdoor way to grab your attention, I wouldn't have let the twins do it."

She leaned. She toppled. "Okay. I forgive you. For this misunderstanding."

"That's an encouraging beginning."

"Beginning? No, not beginning. There's nothing beginning here. I told you three months ago that if you weren't willing to commit yourself to us, then we had come to the final curtain call. You chose to stay in California and, except for last week's spate of packages, share nothing more than phone calls with the kids."

"I called every day at first asking to talk to you. You were the one who refused my calls. I don't think it's so rotten of me to have cut back over the months to keeping up with Kate and Sean a couple times a week. If you had even once just come to the phone..."

Wendie walked across the room and began working with the roses, stripping away the unsalvageable bits to save what she could of the arrangement.

Teague took a step toward her. "Why? Why does it have to be the end? Why can't we have a new beginning?"

"Because nothing has changed." She tore at the battered greenery. "We've just been through too much."

"That sounds to me like an argument to stay together and try to work things out."

She gritted her teeth, wrestled with a stubborn stem, then jumped as a thorn bit into the pad of her thumb. "It's not that easy, Teague. For us to keep our vows, to stay married, would mean we'd have to change so much and—"

"I'm willing to try, Wendie," he whispered.

She turned to face him. "You never give up, do you?"

"Not if it's something I'm passionate about, no. And never where the welfare of the people I love is concerned."

She met his gaze.

He seemed to look straight into her heart, no guile or pretense in his eyes.

She looked away. She didn't know what to say to him. She couldn't even sort through her own thoughts and feelings. Still, something inside her knew she could not let him walk out of here until they'd taken the time to truly talk. "That towel isn't doing any good. The material is soaked through. It should be put in the dryer."

"I have my suitcase in the car. I could go get it and change while these things dry. That is, if you think you could stand to have me around a little while longer?"

Her pulse fluttered. She drew from the tangle of petals, stems, and ferns the only perfect rose to survive the abuse. "Okay. I guess I could stand that. For a little while."

Wendie went about her business. She picked up things left out of place. She gathered the newspaper to neatly bind it up for the recycle bin. She pushed the feather duster around an arrangement of spotless knickknacks. Yet somehow whatever she found to do around the small apartment always took her close to her estranged husband.

"I'm not just here to talk about the reunion show, but I won't pretend I don't hope you'll consider the possibility." Teague extended his arm over the back of her new couch.

He'd changed, then given the twins a fistful of quarters so they could go to the laundry room, buy candy from the vending machine, and wait while his wet clothes dried. Then he'd settled onto the couch as if he belonged there.

"I know this project came out of the blue for you,

Wendie, and that we've talked about it happening before, but it always fell through." He started to put his feet on the coffee table.

She stopped and folded her arms, the bright pink feather duster still in one hand.

He stole a glance at her.

A stab of sadness over all the time they'd spent apart shot through her, but she held her breath and held her ground.

He stretched his legs out, feet under the table, then went on talking. "Those two reasons alone are enough to make you hesitate to even consider it—"

Sadness turned to hurt and disbelief in an instant. "You think that's what this is all about? That I'm reluctant because it caught me off guard, because similar projects have failed to get off the ground before?"

"No. I do know better than that." He met her gaze. Pain flashed in his green eyes. His voice was gruff and strained. "I'm no fool, Wendie. I know you don't want anything to do with the show because you don't want anything to do with me."

"Is that what you really think?" She felt slapped and rushed on to answer her own question. "I can see by the look in your eyes that it is."

"What else should I think?"

"That you have to ask that, that you have no clue as to what went wrong between us, Teague—that's what really hurts the most." Her breath caught in her chest, and tears filled her eyes.

He sat forward, his hand open in a gesture of helplessness.

"When did you stop listening to me? When did our marriage and...and our family stop being the first priority in your heart? When did we start always coming in a distant second to your goals and work?"

He stood. His lips went tight and his face pale. "Working is how I made you and the kids my top priority, by providing for you. What did you want me to do, stop working and stay home with you and the kids twenty-four hours a day?"

"I told you what I wanted not ten seconds ago! I want you to *listen* to me; I want the children and me to be first in your heart. I didn't say anything about you staying with us around the clock. The fact that you immediately turned it into that, that you became defensive instead of responding to what I said, just proves my point. You don't listen to me anymore, Teague."

"It's because I took the soap-opera job without talking to you about it first, isn't it?"

She groaned and threw up her hands.

"I *was* listening to you. I just wanted to give an example of what you're talking about so I could understand what you're talking about."

"I'm talking about communication. I'm talking about putting your own feelings aside and trying to see how your actions affect the ones you love. How about sitting down and explaining what you want? Weigh the consequences in a discussion with me instead of going on a television program and asking in front of the entire country?"

"It's how I asked about the reunion-show deal that you're so upset about?"

"You just don't get it. You aren't even trying to get it."

"Then give me an example. Show me what you mean by putting feelings aside, explaining what you want. All except for the going-on-TV part, I thought I'd done all that."

"Doing it after the fact is not the same thing. Telling someone why you are doing something is not the same thing. Justifying the choices you really wanted to make anyway is not putting your feelings aside. You want an example of what I'm talking about?"

"Yeah, I think it might help because right now I'm—"

"Fine!" She cut him off with a wave of her hand. She could not believe what she was about to offer, but she had to do it. If she wanted to demonstrate to her husband the way she wanted to be treated, she could start with showing him the same consideration. "Here's my example of putting the other person's needs first, of showing a willingness to listen, to work on something together. Give me the script to the reunion movie."

"You'll do it?"

"I'll *read* it."

"Well, that's a start."

"Yes, it is." But what kind of start? Had she just agreed to something that could ultimately heal her family, or would this finally be, as she suspected, the beginning of the end for her marriage?

Three

Wendie's chin dropped to her chest. She startled, disoriented for a second. The rustling of paper in her lap brought her attention back to the script she had agreed to evaluate. She flipped through the remaining pages, yawned, then checked the clock on the table by her bed.

Teague and the kids would be home soon. To give her the peace and quiet to read the script, they'd gone off to a movie and pizza. Thinking about it now, she didn't know who had been more excited about the adventure.

Guilt and frustration nagged at her. Her decision alone had moved the kids so far away from their father. In some ways, she had told herself, she did it for her children's protection. This way she could allow their father to remain a hero in their eyes. Otherwise, his single-mindedness and ambition would slowly sour their relationship.

That excuse did not ease her anxiety much on nights when the children missed their father. Maybe if she could handle this movie situation exactly right, if she could prove to Teague that reason, compromise, and love could work for the good of the whole family...

Then what? Wendie wasn't sure what she hoped to

accomplish. Changing her husband didn't seem likely. But she had promised to read the script, to act on the principles she expected him to embrace.

She wriggled her bare toes, shifted to ease the tension between her shoulders, then scooped up the script. She'd come in here thinking that the privacy of her room, a place where her husband had never been, might help her to focus on the task she'd promised to finish. She reviewed the page she had just fallen asleep reading, then read it again before moving on.

Her opinion of the piece did not improve. She scanned ahead. It only got worse. She sighed, raised the script to eye level, and decided to try speaking a line to see if it sounded as bad as it read. "I can't help it. I love you. I've always loved you. I'm willing to wait for the rest of my life for us to be together, if that's what it takes."

"Oh, I don't think it will take nearly that long."

Teague's amused voice made her jump. She hadn't heard them come in. She hadn't prepared herself to see him leaning against the door to her room.

A roguish grin stole across his lips. His intense eyes fixed on her.

Her defenses went up. She slapped the script into her lap. "It just might take that long before you hear me saying those words, pal."

His face went ashen.

"Those or any other words from this script," she clarified, raising the pages in her hand.

"I know it has a few rough spots, but..."

"No, a Texas horned lizard with a skin condition has a few rough spots. This thing is a disaster."

"It's a made-for-TV reunion movie. You can't expect Shakespeare."

"With this, what you can't expect is an audience."

"On the contrary, one of the cable networks that has had a lot of success with our reruns polled the average viewers. Their data indicates a lot of interest in just this type of project, especially among people our age. In fact, you are probably one of the few people in our demographic group that actually dislikes *The Lost Romance Ranch*."

"What am I supposed to say to that?" She shut her eyes in frustration. "If I contradict you, you'll feel that's some kind of sign that I can be wheedled into doing this movie. If I agree with your assessment, then you'll act hurt and I'll feel bad about that. *Then* you'll wheedle me about doing this show."

"Would it help if I told you I'm at least embarrassed that I'm so easy to predict?" He grinned.

She felt a flutter in her stomach. "Nobody knows you like I do. Too bad that understanding doesn't go both ways. You, of all people, should know how dear the show was to me, how much it *still* means to me."

"I know. I do. It's my frustration talking, that's all." He looked down. "I've missed you so much these past months. And I thought this project might give us a common ground, might bring us back together so we could...work on things."

It hurt to see him humbled like this, but she had to answer what he was saying. "If you wanted to work on making our marriage work, then that's where you need to bring the focus, Teague, not on another business deal that would only make matters worse."

"It wouldn't make matters worse. We'd be working together, don't you see? It wouldn't be about my work taking me away from you; it would be about our building and creating something good and genuine together."

"I thought we *had* built something good and genuine together." An overwhelming ache welled up in her. "Our family."

"We have." He stood straight, his broad shoulders back and his head up. "We have built a wonderful family. What I'm trying to do now is save it."

If only she could believe that. "You're trying to save it by pushing me toward more of what tore us apart?"

"By involving you, the woman I love, in the work that I love."

"I'm not going to go back to working in television. I have a full life, a life I love, homeschooling the kids, volunteering at church, and I hope soon to be working with horses."

"Horses? You mean other than Roanie?"

"Yes. That's why I chose this part of Texas as a place to start over. I've told you all this, you know. I'm hoping to find a little ranch land, maybe board and care for some horses, and even do some work with the disabled, giving them a chance to ride and interact with the animals."

"Sounds like a great dream. And I'm not asking you to abandon it." He moved into the room, slowly, the way Wendie might approach a skittish colt.

"You're not?" She folded her knees to her chest and looped her arms over them.

"I'm only asking you to give me a chance." He moved closer.

She felt hypnotized, drawn by his calm movements, even as her pulse grew rapid and her throat went dry.

"To give *us* a chance." He sat on the edge of the bed and reached toward her. "To give this movie a chance."

She glanced down at his hand atop the open script and blinked. Heat rose in her cheeks. How could she have fallen for his tricks again? "The only chance I am going to give you is that I will give you all the way to the count of three to get out of my home before I pick up the phone and call the police."

"But, Wendie, I—"

"One."

"I don't see why we can't—"

"Two." She stretched her hand toward the phone on the bedside table.

"Okay, I'm going. But I'm leaving the script, and I'm leaving you with this thought: You, the kids—our marriage and family—have always been my first priority."

She pursed her lips but didn't say a thing.

"Maybe I don't act on it in the ways you have decided I should, but I show it in the ways I know how. I show it through hard work, financial support, and loyalty."

"Which is appreciated, but—"

"And I never so much as threatened to walk out on you and the kids."

She held her breath.

"Maybe I haven't worked on things according to your grand design, but I am trying. The fact that I am here proves I am trying, Wendie, not running away from our problems."

She watched him go, her head reeling. She'd agreed to

read the script to teach her husband a lesson. Now, in his one parting sentence, he'd left her feeling as though she was the one who had much to learn.

Teague hunkered down behind the steering wheel of his car and watched the lights go out one by one in the windows of his family's apartment. Cold gripped him despite the warmth of the Texas night. He couldn't remember ever having felt so alone.

It went against his nature to be excluded from anything that he wanted badly. Even when his career had faltered and no one in the business returned his phone calls, he'd hustled and gotten work. He did not take no as an answer then, and he would not take it now, not even from Wendie. She would not shut him out of her life, out of the lives of their children, without a fight. He just had to find a way back into her heart, her good graces. Right now, he'd settle for just getting back into her apartment.

He'd started to reach her. He just knew it. If only he had some time, like the time it would take them to make the movie, he could win her back.

A sharp tapping startled him from his thoughts. A beam of light slashed across his face, making him squint to see past it into the darkness. The glint of a silver badge on a black uniform caught him by surprise.

Wendie had actually called the police. Suddenly his bright hopes for reconciliation dimmed considerably. He rolled down his car window. "Is there some kind of problem, Officer?"

"You have a reason to be in this neighborhood, sir?"

"I, um, I was just visiting someone in this apartment building."

"Uh-huh. Got any identification?" Slowly the officer lowered his flashlight and extended his open hand to accept Teague's license.

"California." He sort of snorted the state name as if he knew something unsavory about the place.

"Yeah, just visiting. From California. I rented the car, but there are papers in the glove compartment, if you need to see—"

"Teague? What kind of name is that?"

"My mother's maiden name." In friendlier circumstances he would have cajoled the man with the story of how he'd had to drop his first name when he joined the union—they already had a John Blackwell on the rolls. Then he would have used his impeccable sense of timing to match his famous dazzling grin with the inevitable sound of recognition. Right now he dared not chance it. If Wendie had called the police, the man knew enough about him already. If she hadn't, he wanted to protect her privacy any way he could.

"Hmm. Teague Blackwell. Can't get over how I think I've heard that name before. Not from around here?"

"No sir."

"Huh." He shook his head. "Well, either way, you're illegally parked."

So Wendie hadn't called. He sighed. "Um, sorry about that. I didn't know. If it matters, I didn't see any sign."

"Right there." The officer pointed. "Only going to give you a warning, since you're from out of state. Don't get many out-of-staters through here anymore. Not since they put in the bypasses and old Route 66 got all...That's it!"

Teague winced.

"You're that guy!" He pointed with his pen. "From the TV, from that show, that ranch right around these parts!"

"*The Lost Romance Ranch.*" The grin was pure reflex.

Before he knew what hit him, Teague was sitting on the hood of his car, signing autographs to every person in Officer Drake's family, neighborhood, and Sunday school class.

~

Wendie couldn't sleep. Emotions running high, she'd told herself. But when she had walked to her window fully expecting to gaze up at the moon and have a nice long talk with the Lord about it, she had seen the true cause for her restlessness. In moments she had thrown her light summer robe on over her nightgown and dashed outside to see what kind of mayhem her husband had created now.

"Make this one to Cissy. She had the biggest crush on you." Officer Drake glanced up and nodded.

Wendie padded barefoot to the curb, relying on her porch light and the illumination spilling from Teague's open car door to light the way. The officer, whose gruff exterior hid a big friendly teddy bear of a man, looked like a kid in a candy store as he collected the autographs. He appeared so taken, in fact, that he didn't even seem to notice her approach with anything more than a quick glance.

"Hey there, Wendie, did you know we had an honest-to-goodness celebrity visiting our town?"

She opened her mouth to say something, then reconsidered. She only knew Officer Drake through the church she'd been attending over the summer. She wasn't even sure he knew her last name. If he did, his excitement over meeting a celebrity seemed to have temporarily displaced it. If neither she nor Teague said anything to jar his memory, her secret might remain safe.

"An *honest-to-goodness* celebrity, you say?" She gave Teague a warning look.

Her husband gave her a pained smile and handed Drake the paper he'd just signed.

"Now make one out for Bob and Nadine." The officer pointed to the pad in Teague's hand, then pointed to the man himself. "This fellow was on that old TV show set in these parts. That's why I have to get so many autographs. You know, folks around here just loved that show."

"Lots of people did and still do." Teague handed the pen and paper to the other man, but the message he was delivering was for Wendie, and she knew it.

"This is a new lady in town—goes to my church." Drake stretched his hand toward Wendie. "She probably doesn't even realize she's living in a town on the edge of a little stretch of old Route 66. We're just a stone's throw from the old Flying C Dude Ranch; lots of people think it was the ranch in your show."

She *hadn't* realized that when she chose this town, though she did know about the ranch on the edge of town. The rumor that the Flying C might be for sale was one of the things that had drawn her to move here and enroll the kids in a weeklong camp. Knowing the place had a link to *The Lost Romance Ranch* might have made her think twice about both those decisions. "I thought Route 66 ran by the Double Heart Diner northwest of here."

"It did, but it curved along this way, too. Doesn't run through town but veers off along the north side." He jerked his thumb in the general direction of a nearly deserted stretch of road that framed the outskirts of town.

"I think I drove past that coming in today. Where a row of run-down motor courts and motels are all boarded up?"

"Yep." He turned to Teague. " 'Course now, there isn't but the one place to stay the night in town, the Yellow Rose Inn. Only fair to warn you though, you being a visiting celebrity and all, that everyone likes to keep an eye on that place."

"Really?"

"To make sure no one from town has a car parked there that should be home in the driveway, if you know what I mean."

"Sounds like it's a regular local attraction." Teague looked from Drake to Wendie. "That could present a problem."

"No." She said it. She certainly *thought* she said it. Her mouth moved, but no sound came out.

"Now, I can't say you have to use an alias, but I can say that a standout name like Teague Blackwell is gonna command some attention."

"Just like the man it belongs to," Wendie muttered.

"And pretty quick, someone's gonna put two and two

together. Right, Ms. Blackwell—" His jaw dropped and he let out a low groan.

Wendie winced.

"I cannot believe I missed that connection. You two related?"

"We're..." She glanced at her husband. She'd never said these words aloud before, but she felt she had to make the situation very clear—to everyone. "We're separated."

Teague opened his mouth, then shut it and looked away.

Wendie pushed aside the rush of conflicting emotions all this had caused in her and smiled at the officer. "It's a long story that I'd rather not go into, if you don't mind."

"Oh. Yeah, sure." Drake looked genuinely concerned. Then his brow pleated and his jaw set. He glowered at Teague, sizing him up, then turned to Wendie. "Are you all right? Do you need some kind of police protection?"

Wendie cocked her head, trying to think where that odd question had come from, then it dawned on her. "Oh no, no. Teague was just leaving after a visit with the twins. He's not a stalker or anything like that."

"Good. So you're in town to see your kids, huh?" He turned to Teague.

Wendie tensed, willing him not to bring up that movie deal or anything that might stir the man's memory further. Something that might make him realize that she, too, had been in "that show" that he recalled so fondly.

"Just a short visit, I assure you." Teague's gaze shifted to her, then back to the officer. "In a day or two I'll be back on the road and..."

"Good. A day or two, huh? I know a lot of people who would love to meet you in person, lots of fans in these parts, like I said. Maybe the café could throw a barbecue in your honor, if I got the word out..."

"You can't tell a soul about my being here." Teague spoke before she could. "In fact I'd rather you didn't share those autographs with anyone for a while, long enough for Wendie to come up with a plan for handling anyone else who might make the connection."

She blinked, unsure she could trust her ears. Had her husband just chosen her feelings over what he had always seen as his obligation to his fans?

"Our first consideration has to be Wendie and the twins and their peace of mind, don't you agree?"

"Yes, yes, I see that." Drake went back to his cruiser and opened the door. "You can count on me to keep quiet about it all, then. Don't forget to move your car."

"I will."

"And keep in mind what I said about the Yellow Rose Inn not being the best place for keeping your whereabouts a secret."

"Thank you, Officer."

"Thank you, Officer Drake. We'll see you in church." Wendie waved like she hadn't a care in the world. When, in fact, she felt as if the world had just settled its weight on her shoulders.

Teague could not stay at the Yellow Rose Inn. He certainly couldn't drive out to the dude ranch and see if they had a vacancy. Either action would simply bring too much attention. There was a third possibility. A few hours ago she would never have allowed herself to contemplate it.

"Well, I guess I'd better get going." He started to lower himself into his car, then stopped and stood again, laying both his arms atop the open door. "I hope you know that if I'd suspected my coming here would stir up a lot of problems for you and the kids, I'd never have done it. Whatever you may think of my style of showing it, I do love you all, with all my heart. I'd never knowingly hurt you."

Wendie pressed her lips together. She wanted to tell him again that his very unawareness of how his rash decisions, based on his own needs and goals, hurt them all was the exact reason she had finally left their marriage. But why go over that again and again? It never seemed to make any difference.

Or had it? Teague's words to Officer Drake echoed in her thoughts. *You can't tell a soul about my being here. Our first consideration has to be Wendie and the twins and their peace of mind...* Had she finally, after all this time, had some kind of impact? Had their separation given Teague the jolt he needed to want to do better?

"If you were really worried about how your presence would affect us, you'd have mailed that script." She folded her arms.

"I pursued that deal because I thought it could bring us together, Wendie." His voice was raw. "That was foremost in my mind. It's always been in my heart since the day you left."

In the dim light she studied his face for any signs of insincerity.

The car's interior light made his features seem more lined and weary than she'd ever seen them. His eyes did not shine with merriment. His strong shoulders slumped. "I am willing to work on things, Wendie, but that takes time. Time is the one thing you don't seem willing to give me. It's one thing I thought this project could provide. That's why I wanted to bring it to you in person, because I knew you'd never take the time to consider it otherwise."

She looked in his kind, tired eyes, and suddenly her heart filled. She swallowed back a moment of shame for letting her own fear and hardness keep her from realizing that she hadn't given him a real second chance, this man she'd vowed to love and honor for all her life. She could not go forward with anything as destructive as breaking up a family without giving their marriage every opportunity to survive. She'd keep her guard up, but she had to open her mind and heart to all possibilities. She had to open her mind, heart, and *home.*

"I will probably regret this before your stay is over, and I don't want you reading too much into it, but..." She stole a peek over her shoulder at the place she had meant as her haven from the influence of this very man, then sighed.

"Are you suggesting I stay with you?" The old energy infused his tone again.

She tugged her robe closed all the way to the neck. "The couch in the living room pulls out into a bed."

"Fine. Good. Thanks."

She pivoted on her heel and hurried back across the lawn, calling after her, "You can park in the extra slot for my apartment; it's marked in the lot. If you need anything, look around. Don't bother trying to ask me where to find it."

"Why not?"

She turned and gave him one last look. "Because I'll be in my room, banging my head against the locked door for being such a soft touch."

She wasn't sure because her heartbeat was pounding so loudly in her ears, but she thought she heard him answer, "You won't regret this, Wendie. I promise."

As she slipped through her front door, she murmured a silent prayer that her husband was right and asked the Lord to guide her decisions about this, as she no longer trusted her own judgment.

Four

Do you think he's going to sleep all day?"

A soft buzzing invaded his dreams. He seemed to hear his young daughter.

"I think he's dead."

And his son.

"He's not dead. Dead men don't snore like hibernating bears with a bad case of sinusitis."

And Wendie. But then, Wendie was a regular in his dreams, though she usually said much kinder things.

"He's smiling. Does that mean he's waking up?"

"I think it means we should go back into the kitchen and wait for him to wake up on his own," Wendie whispered.

Teague stirred. Wendie was leaving—another recurring feature in far too many of his dreams. He thrashed in the sheets, trying to reach out to her, to follow, calling out as he battled the covers, "Don't go, Wendie."

He heard her quietly instruct the children to go ahead and start breakfast while she talked to their father. He felt the metal frame of the foldout mattress wobble and then list to one side as she settled on the edge of the bed.

"I'm here." She touched his shoulder lightly, her

knuckles brushing his neck. "I'm not going anywhere."

He cupped his hand over hers and drew her palm up along his bristled jaw. He opened his eyes, half expecting her to vanish and leave him with the realization that he was alone and all but lost without her.

She smiled at him.

He sat up, her hand still in his. "I was dreaming, I think. I had this vision of you leaving me, and me searching for you and not being able to find you again. I hate that dream."

"Me, too," she said, so softly he almost wondered if she'd actually spoken.

He wanted to ask her if she meant she had those dreams too, but he doubted she'd admit it. And if she did admit it, then what? Everything hung in such a delicate balance right now. If he suggested they did not have to lose each other at all, that they could fall into one another's arms and hang on for dear life, she might balk and throw her defenses up again. Each time she did that, Teague could feel his hope of reconciliation slipping further and further away.

He cleared his throat. "Thanks for waking me up."

"You were snoring. That's a sure sign of age, you know."

"Hey, I can't deny it, I'm not as young as I used to be."

"Who is?" She put a hand to her cheek. "I wake up with such a puffy face some mornings I look like a chipmunk storing up food for winter."

"You? Never!" He took her hand away so he could just sit and savor the sight of her beautiful eyes and heartwarming smile. "You'll always seem eighteen to me, Wendie."

"And you'll always seem about twelve to me." She lifted her head, acting cool and untouched by his compliment, but her eyes sparkled.

At least this defense came in good humor, he thought. He ran his fingers along the side of his head where his hair had begun to go silver. "Hey, now, a little respect for your elders, please."

"You're only a couple years older than me, pal, and graying hair notwithstanding, you're far from an elder."

"Gray hair is a crown of splendor; it is attained by a righteous life."

"Who says?" She laughed.

"Proverbs 16:31 says, young lady."

"You and your amazing memory. Even when we were kids you had learned everyone's lines in a few readings." She shook her head. "And you always could cite chapter and verse to apply to any situation."

"Maybe that's because, no matter what the situation, there always *is* an answer in the Bible." That should send a clear message without too much pushing. It would remind Wendie that they had an obligation to God, each other, and their children to work things out. It reminded them both of where to seek good counsel to help them do just that.

"I know. And I know that's your not-so-subtle way of telling me that a divorce will hurt more than just you and me." Her eyes glistened with unshed tears. She bowed her head just enough to hide her face from him. "I…I just don't know what to do about all this."

"Don't cry." He edged forward, taking her chin in his hand. "I can't stand it when you cry. I'm sorry for getting into this first thing. Haven't even been awake fifteen minutes, and I'm already pushing you to deal with our situation. Can you forgive me?"

"Thank you for recognizing I'm not ready to talk about this." She leaned forward, one hand on his shoulder, and placed the other gently on his cheek. "You have no idea what that means to me."

As she pulled away, their gazes met.

He looked deeply into the eyes of the woman he loved but so often simply did not understand, wishing he knew what more to say. Saying anything at all would be too much, so he did the thing that was in his heart.

He kissed his wife. Gently, not grabbing at her or pulling her close but with all the tenderness and longing of their first kiss so many years ago. And she did not stop him.

She kept her hands on his shoulders, as if she might at any moment shove him away, but she did not retreat from him. That simple gesture gave him more hope than he had felt in months.

"Wow, Katie, you have got to see this!"

"Mom! Dad!"

"Oh, I... This isn't what you think, kids." Wendie leapt up from beside her husband. She had not meant to let him kiss her. But after he'd once again shown that he could put her feelings first, she had been confused and...and she had wanted to kiss him. That was the truth of it; she had wanted to kiss her husband.

Now she had to deal with the effects that moment of

self-indulgence might have on her children. It wasn't a promise of reconciliation, after all, and she had to let her children and her husband know that. "Back to the kitchen, you two. I'll be in to talk to you in a minute."

"I thought she was just going to wake him up," Katie whispered loudly as the pair hurried off.

"Well, maybe that's why Dad spent the night here instead of the local motel," Sean countered, not even bothering with the pretense of a whisper. "Better wake-up service!"

"Don't you dare," Wendie warned the man smirking up at her from the rumpled sofa bed. "Not even so much as one snicker."

"Me?" He gave her that practiced expression of total innocence.

She clenched her jaw. She'd seen that look on him in response to everything from being caught putting empty milk cartons back in the fridge to unannounced business trips that ran roughshod over her feelings in pursuit of his own goals. Seeing it now did not ease the knot in her stomach. "I think your staying here is a bad idea. In fact, you shouldn't have come here at all. I think it's time you went back to California."

"What about the..."

She tensed. She was asking him to leave, and his first priority was going to be that awful script.

"Twins?" he finished softly.

"What?"

"I haven't seen them in so long. I've come all this way. If nothing else, don't cut my time short with them. Please."

Who is this man? she wondered, her emotions twisting

inside her like a rag through a wringer. Could her husband really have changed so much? Had the separation made him finally assess what mattered most to him? Or was this a roundabout tactic to get things done his way?

Standing there looking into those compelling, sincere eyes, she could not decide. "Why don't you get dressed, and we can talk about this over coffee?"

By the time he had showered and shaved, the kids were on kitchen duty and Wendie was nowhere in sight.

"There's coffee over here, Daddy." Katie pointed with her chin as she rinsed plates and glasses, then put them in the dishwasher.

Sean was working away, slopping a damp mop over the small vinyl floor. Still, he was not too occupied to crack, "Yeah, try some coffee, Dad. It'll really wake you up."

"Not funny," he warned, in no mood for teasing about the kiss he'd shared with Wendie.

Sean hung his head, obviously embarrassed at his father's gentle rebuke.

"You missed a spot." Teague pointed downward.

"Where?" Sean squinted.

Teague just tapped the floor with the toe of his leather running shoe.

Sean mopped his way over to his dad's side. "I don't see it. Where?"

Teague pointed to the floor again. "Right there."

He brought his hand up to brush his fingertip past his son's nose.

The second the boy knew he'd been had, Teague wrapped him in a bear hug and began to play at wrestling with him.

Sean groaned, but his body shook with laughter, and he did not fight to get away. The awkwardness about his joke over Wendie's wake-up kiss dissipated, and the boy went back to work.

"That coffee smells great." Teague opened a cabinet and peered in at the neat stacks of canned goods. He shut that door with a bang, then opened another and then another, unable to locate what he needed.

"The coffee mugs, creamer, and sugar are in the cabinet above the coffeemaker." Katie dripped water across the counter as she pointed.

"Thanks." He gave his girl a wink as he crossed the room, but underneath the facade he felt frustrated and ill at ease. He chose a yellow cup with the words *World's Greatest Mom* on it, knowing it was Wendie's favorite. Just holding something she cherished gave him some measure of comfort. He poured the steaming brew, added creamer and sugar, then realized he had no idea which drawer held the silverware.

Heavy sadness settled over him. He wanted to know where to find things in his family's home. Even a casual acquaintance would probably know where to find a cup or spoon in this place, but he was an outsider among the people he loved most in the world.

"Done with the kitchen floor." Sean wrung the mop out. "C'mon, Katie, help me vacuum the carpets, and we'll have our chores done for the day."

The kids hurried out, each trying to get in front of the

other as they argued over who got to vacuum which room. He watched them go just as Wendie came to the door.

His heart thudded hard in his ears at the sight of her. He wanted to be a part of her life again, to find a way to make her happy. He prayed it was possible to do both.

"Who owes who an apology?" Venturing into the room, she clutched the script to her chest like a shield.

"Me, to you. I was out of line from the start, just showing up like I did. Then the whole incident with Officer Drake, and the kiss..."

"I can't let you take the entire blame for the last one. And for the rest, well, I haven't exactly been fair or open to the situation." She tucked a strand of soft brown hair behind her ear. "Guess the question is, what are we going to do about it?"

He ached to go to her, but he made himself stand still. He leaned back against the kitchen counter, his coffee cup in one hand. "Too late to start over?"

"I'm afraid to ask how you mean that."

"You tell me."

She shifted her feet, looked over her shoulder toward the sound of the vacuum cleaner humming in another room, then splayed her hand over the pages pressed to her chest. "What say we start with this thing and see how that goes?"

"You mean that?" He pushed away from the counter but did not go to her. "You want to talk about doing the movie?"

"I'm willing to talk about the *script*, yes. Beyond that, well..."

"It's a start." He gestured toward the tiny kitchen table. "I'd love to hear what you think."

"I think I'm hearing things." She grinned at him as she stepped fully into the room. "But I like what I'm hearing."

Two cups of coffee later, the kids had scooted off with a neighbor and her children to the pool. Teague was seated at the table with his feet in the chair beside him while Wendie paced back and forth like a lawyer in closing argument.

"In the end, it just doesn't hold up. It's stale. How can you ask me to go back to this tired, stereotyped role?" She held the script up in one hand. "Did these writers crawl out of a time warp or something?"

"I don't follow you on that. Can you give me an example?"

"Okay, one thing that drove me absolutely crazy—everyone kept referring to Claire as an old maid."

"A couple times, four at the most."

"It doesn't matter how many times they said it. No one is an old maid anymore. It's corny. And she's thirty-five, not even all that old, really." She gave a glance that seemed to ask him for backup.

"It's young, really."

"Far too young to be depicted as this sad, lonely creature who has entirely given up on love."

"True."

"I'm that age, and I certainly haven't given up on..."

It took a lot of control for him not to prod her to say more. *What have you not given up on, Wendie? Love in a general sense or love between the two of us?* But he remained quiet, his expression neutral. "Is that your only complaint with the story line?"

"No. There are..." She flipped through the pages, but her focus was clearly not on the script. "There are lots of things. I can't pinpoint them right now, but it's got a lot of flaws. It's not believable."

"Believable?" He laughed. "Honey, it's a reunion movie based on a show about an angel, keeping watch over a stretch of Route 66 and the family on a run-down ranch who befriend him. Where did you think *believable* worked into that picture?"

"Okay, I'll give you that."

"Good."

"But even you have to admit that it's a bit dated. Times have changed. Attitudes have changed. You can't expect people to embrace characters who haven't changed with them."

Teague sloshed the cold dregs of his coffee around in his cup. "You can't mess with success. This formula worked. It still works in reruns for a large audience. Why don't you tell me what's really bothering you about this story? It's the romance between our two characters, isn't it?"

"No...well, yes." She sighed, her brown eyes intense and her full lips not quite in a frown. "Okay, yes—but not for the reasons you're assuming."

"I'm not assuming anything." He held his hands out, palms up, as if showing her he had nothing to hide. "Why don't you tell me your reasons?"

She nodded, strode away one more time, then turned. "Aside from the pure silliness of the whole angel-earning-the-right-to-become-a-human-for-the-sake-of-love thing..."

"A contrivance, to be sure. But a much-used, much-*loved* contrivance. And part of the show from way back, if not the very beginning," he reminded her.

"Okay, granted. And it's even not so bad that the plot does tie up some loose ends, centering on Ryder the angel finally doing enough good deeds to earn his humanity."

"But?"

"But it's my character, like I said. She's so...pathetic." Wendie slumped her shoulders forward and let her shiny golden brown hair fall into her eyes for effect.

Teague laughed. "She's not that pathetic."

Wendie shook her hair back. "She has lived her whole life on that ranch, barely getting by, while every other character has gone on with life. And why is she hanging around without any life to speak of? She's hoping that your character will, after twenty years, finally see how much she loves him?"

"And realize how much he loves her," he added softly.

"It's pathetic."

"It's pivotal."

"To what?" Suspicion colored her voice.

"To summing up the whole story, to giving the viewers what they want, what they have wanted since you and I took on those roles as teenagers." He dropped his feet to the floor.

Her brow furrowed, and she shook her head.

"Don't you get it, Wendie?" He set his caution aside now and went to her, taking her by the shoulders in his strong but gentle grasp. "You and I are the lost romance of *The Lost Romance Ranch.*"

"We are?" Her eyes told him she wanted to believe that.

"Our characters embody that lost romance." And in a sense, they themselves did too. They had lost the romance that had once enlivened their marriage. But they could get it back. He knew they could, if they would both just try a little harder to make this work. "All those years our characters lived an impossible situation. Caring for each other, wanting to have that proverbial happily-ever-after, but knowing it couldn't be unless..."

"Unless the writers intervened." She smiled. "So you're saying fans of the show would really go for this plot line?"

"Everyone wants us back together. That is, they want our characters to get together."

"I just can't believe that anyone would..."

"Don't take my word for it. Why not ask them?"

"Oh sure. You saw how Officer Drake acted around you. What if he realized that some lady who goes to his church used to be on 'that ranch show' too? Be realistic, Teague, I can't go around polling locals on something like that."

"Then why not take it on the road?"

She put her face in her hands. "I know I'll regret asking this, but what are you talking about?"

"Just so happens that I have a string of personal appearances lined up along what's left of Route 66 between here and Santa Fe."

"You do?"

"Yes. Remember when that author, David Penn, contacted me awhile back to do a foreword to a book he was writing on the Mother Road?"

"Yes." Her back stiffened. "As I recall, you locked yourself away in your study every night for a week trying to get it just right."

He hadn't meant to bring up another sore spot. But then he had not realized this was a sore spot. Could he really have been that blind to the ways he had been shutting his family out? "I guess I got so caught up in the writing I didn't think about how you might feel about it. You...you don't resent the book or anything because of that, do you?"

"That would be pretty petty of me, wouldn't it?" She folded her arms.

"Good. Because he's doing some book signings along Route 66 and I said I'd join up with him when I could. Also I have some promos lined up for stations airing reruns, that kind of thing."

"So that's the real reason you came out to Texas?"

"No. I told you the real reason I'm here—you and the kids. The appearances are just some things Penn and I have thrown together, places along the way in the drive back to California."

"I see."

"Why don't you and the kids come with me, and you can ask the fans yourself how they feel about our characters having a romance? I'd sure welcome your company."

"Oh, I just bet you would." She narrowed her eyes at him.

He stepped away from her, afraid she'd interpret any contact as trying to sway things in his favor. Still, he buzzed with excitement at the idea of a summer road trip with the ones he loved and had missed so much. "C'mon,

Wendie, don't you want to go out and meet your public again after all this time?"

"I don't have a public. I have a family. I have responsibilities to the children. What if it all turns out badly? I can't drag them along and risk having them see everything fall apart before their eyes."

"What if it doesn't fall apart, Wendie? What if it gives us the chance to rebuild our life together and be a family again?"

Her gaze searched his. She laced her fingers together. "You're sure we are the lost romance in *The Lost Romance Ranch?* Our characters, I mean?"

"Positive." He lifted her chin with one knuckle. Risky as it seemed, he knew that he had to push things now—just a little—or possibly lose everything. "But it doesn't have to be that way, Wendie. We can find romance again. We can find the love we used to share not so long ago. Come with me, and let's try."

"The kids are scheduled for a weeklong summer camp. I suppose..."

"Yes! You could come with me and then you wouldn't feel you'd dragged the kids into the middle of things. When is the camp?" He reached into the back pocket of his jeans to get his wallet and the card calendar he carried in it.

"Whoa! Slow down, there. I didn't say I'd go. This cannot work if you try to bulldoze me into this."

Slowly, he put his wallet back and held his hands up. "My mistake. Old habits and all."

She glowered at him.

"This approach to our relationship is still a little new

to me. Can't expect perfection every time from the get-go." He grinned, then added, "Not even from me."

Her glower softened.

"Why don't I take the kids out this afternoon and give you some time to think about this in private?"

She sighed, shut her eyes, then nodded. "Okay. I'm not promising things will work out the way you hope, but I will think it over."

"That's all I ask, Wendie. That's all I ask."

Five

"I love you, you know."

"We know, Dad." Katie and Sean rolled their eyes in unison. At twelve, they no longer welcomed the public display of affection by a parent.

"Okay, okay!" Teague held up his hands. "I just wanted to make sure you knew that your mom and I not being together right now has nothing to do with our feelings about you two."

He glanced around the Double Heart Diner, an old café left over from the boom days of Route 66 that was now undergoing major renovations. The updates seemed to have done the trick: The place was bustling with diners, three waitresses, two cooks, and a woman working the cash register with a bouffant hairdo the shape and consistency of varnished cotton candy.

He watched his two dark-haired children gobbling down greasy fries and enormous hamburgers. Like this place, while the essentials stayed the same, subtle changes in his children signaled to him that things could never go back to the way they once were. A fleeting pang of regret over their lost time caught him off guard. "You know, guys, I just realized that even in the short time since I last saw you, you've grown, matured."

"Gee, Dad, I was about to say the same thing 'bout you." Sean grinned and pushed a crinkled fry through a pool of catsup on his plate.

He chuckled. "Guess you two think your old dad is a great big goofball for getting all sentimental like that, don't you?"

"That's not why we think you're a goofball." The boy popped the fry in his mouth.

"Quit it, Sean." Katie elbowed her brother lightly in the ribs.

"No fighting, you two," Teague warned in his Dad-knows-best tone. "Sean, there's been an obvious undercurrent of hostility between you and me the whole time I've been visiting."

His son seemed suddenly intent on his dinner.

"I think something is bothering you."

Sean stuffed a fry into his mouth.

"I also think you have matured since the last time we really talked. So let's handle it that way. If you have something to say to me, say it outright."

"Honest?" He gulped down his food, then took a sip of his soft drink.

"I wouldn't have it any other way."

"Okay." Sean gave his sister a quick glance, then narrowed his eyes on Teague. "I do think you're a big goofball because you let Mom leave. You let her move us all the way out to Texas, and you didn't come too."

"I had the contract with the soap opera, son, and..." He looked into his children's eyes, and the excuse sounded lame even to him. He ran his fingers along the rim of his glass of iced tea and sighed. "Is that how you feel too, Katie?"

"I don't think it was right for Mom to leave and take us away," she said firmly. Then her green eyes fixed on him with the unflinching candor of a child's wounded heart. "But you stayed away too long. Mom left because she thought work meant more to you than we did and...well, after you didn't come for so long, it was hard not to start believing she was right."

"No, Katie, I don't feel that way. I love you two and Mom more than anything." He reached over and took her hand in his. "It's because of you that I work so hard."

"You like the work," Sean muttered.

"Yes, to be totally fair, I have to admit, I do like the work. I like the feeling that I'm doing something that touches other people's lives in a positive way."

"How?"

"Well, as a celebrity, even a minor one, I can be an example of a godly person. You know, a candle in the darkness kind of thing."

"What about the example we need in our lives?" Katie whispered.

He swallowed hard, but the lump in his throat didn't budge. He drew in as deep a breath as his tight chest allowed and tried to explain. "From my vantage point, I was being an example to you kids. I had a contractual obligation. If I walked out on my contract, I wouldn't be able to get work again. The kind of work I do, it's easy to fall from favor and never get another job. That's what I do to provide for this family."

"Mom says there are residuals and investments. That

there's enough to buy a business and still have plenty left over." Sean folded his arms.

"Those are for the future, for a time when I can't get work anymore and..." Teague leaned forward, his forearms against the edge of the table. "You sure know a lot more about the family's finances than you used to."

"Mom didn't want us to worry that after we left we'd suddenly go hungry or anything." Sean shrugged, no doubt trying to play it as matter-of-fact, grown-up conversation. "And then when she started looking at the old ranch, she told us—"

"She told us it would be a great place for us to go to summer camp," Katie rushed in to say.

"Your mom is seriously thinking about investing in a recreational ranch?"

"She just looked at it," Katie said, her eyes full of innocence and a look of someone who might have said too much but wasn't sure.

"You know how she likes horses." Sean plunged into his burger with much more gusto than the greasy fare warranted.

They say you learn more from your children than they do from you. Teague had learned quite a lot in the last few minutes, including this tidbit about Wendie and a horse ranch. Very interesting indeed. Also, he thought sadly, he knew now that, while he had believed his actions were teaching the twins about the work ethic and honoring commitments, that was not the lesson they had learned.

Teague sat back in the booth and stared out at the weathered strip of old Route 66 that ran past the diner.

He'd come here to convince Wendie to work things out his way—and seen that his way was just what stood between them.

He'd behaved according to conscientious guiding principles for his children's sake and discovered his children felt hurt by that very action. He'd hoped down deep that this movie deal, and then later the promotional trip, would win his wife over and bring her and the children back to California.

But Wendie had designs on a ranch in Texas. He could hardly take it all in or decide what he should do about any of it. Ironically, he had gone off with the kids to give Wendie time to think, but this afternoon had certainly left him with plenty to consider as well.

The house was too quiet. Wendie went to the window and peered out. As much as she'd appreciated the peace and quiet and time to think, the things she had thought of in the stillness of her strange new apartment had not brought her any closer to a decision.

What Teague had asked of her seemed perilously close to giving in to the old way of doing things. He'd made the plans without her input. It was for his project, for the good of his career, but even she could see how, if it worked, this could benefit the whole family as well.

She could not forget the changes she'd seen in the man, his willingness to try to do better, to listen to her, to take her feelings into account. Her mind had replayed again and again the many ways he seemed genuinely sincere in his desire to repair their marriage. And she could not stop thinking about that kiss.

Wendie put her fingertips to her lips. As vividly as the instant it happened, she felt the power of his gaze in her eyes, the strength of his shoulders beneath her hands, the touch of his lips on hers. She felt a flush on her cheeks, and she sighed like a lovesick teenager. That a simple kiss from her own husband of fifteen years could affect her so made her smile, and made her stomach knot. Was she too much of an emotional mess to make the right decision?

She did not believe in divorce, but she'd felt she had to protect her children from Teague's growing emotional indifference to what was best for them. God had given her a dilemma fit for Solomon, and even though she had prayed over it, she had not come up with the wisdom to handle it beyond knowing that she must do as she expected her husband to do. She must put the needs of others first, primarily the children.

Deciding to let their needs guide her in this matter, Wendie moved away from the window and headed for the kitchen to get a cold drink. She hadn't taken more than two steps when the front door flew open with a bang. She gasped and spun around.

Two black-haired tornadoes went screaming by, their feet thundering even on the carpeted floor. As they tore past, one of them pressed a spray can into her hand. They both ducked behind her, using her body like a shield.

A hissing sound drew her attention back to the open doorway. "What is—"

A jet of cold, plastic-smelling string came out of no-where to tangle at her throat. She shrieked and snatched it away just as the sight of Teague's face registered in her mind.

He darted across the doorway, practically begging for retaliation.

Without warning, the twins blasted pink and orange fluorescent streamers past her head.

"Ha! Missed me!" Teague laughed.

Wendie stared at twin globs of drying aerosol string dripping down the eggshell-colored walls beside her door.

"Shoot the string, Mom." Sean raised her hand with the uncapped can in it.

"It comes right off when it dries," Katie assured her.

Teague burst into the room, his spray can at the ready.

"Do it now, Mom," Sean yelled. "It's us against him."

The words struck Wendie in the heart. That kind of thinking was exactly what she had wanted to avoid when she brought the children to Texas. She had not wanted them to endure feeling that they weren't a real team anymore, that they no longer tried to work together. She made up her mind in that instant. She saw what she had to do, for herself and most of all for her children.

Teague advanced on them.

"Get him for us, Mom," the twins urged in unison.

"What do you mean 'us,' short persons?" Wendie pivoted, her index finger on the nozzle, and pushed. The can sputtered and spit out only a short splatter of broken string.

"Mine doesn't work," she protested.

"Don't worry, Wendie. I'll save you!" A strong arm circled her waist from behind, and the twins stumbled backward under a barrage of pale blue goo. As Teague dragged her toward the kitchen, he took her spray can and jerked it back and forth a few times. "Sometimes you have to shake it up to get it working right."

"Just like life, huh?"

"I guess you could say that." He handed her the can as he propelled her sideways to duck behind the sofa.

She missed the handoff, and the cylinder of string rolled into the middle of the room.

"Cover me. I'm going after your weapon." He gave her his string, then lifted her chin with one finger and hammed it up big-time as he told her, "It's our only hope."

The children's squeals interrupted what might have been a moment of tenderness amid the tomfoolery. His lips brushed her cheek all too lightly.

"I'm going for it, baby."

In the hokey old-style gangster accent he used, Wendie couldn't tell if he meant he was going for a real kiss or the spray can. Without thinking, she wet her lips, but he had already lurched away from her.

She couldn't help but laugh out loud at the way he put one hundred and ten percent into everything he committed himself to do.

"Don't worry about me." Crouching, he glanced over his shoulder at her. "I did this once as a guest star on a cop show and..."

"Would you go already?" She nudged him with the toe of her tennis shoe.

He hurled his body in the direction of the abandoned canister.

Wendie rose up from the safety of the sofa and took

aim. Her can coughed out a pathetic drizzle of string. "Wait! I didn't get it…"

The hissing of compressed air filled the air from the twins' direction.

Teague let out a strangled groan, then fell with a thud in the middle of the room. He lay there belly up, with snarls of obnoxious string drying in masses on his chest, arms, and legs.

"Oh no!" Wendie tossed her can to the floor and swept across the room to his side. She fell to her knees and cradled his head in her lap. "Forgive me, darling." She let out an overplayed sigh, allowed for a melodramatic pause, then concluded, "I forgot to shake."

Teague gasped for air, flailed his legs, then clutched his chest.

The twins laughed.

Wendie laughed.

Teague opened one eye, caught her attention, and winked.

Her heart soared. For just that one moment they felt like a family again. She knew she had to try to do whatever it took to make that a real possibility.

"We won! We won!" The twins leapt in the air, high-fiving each other.

Wendie stood and offered her hand to her husband. "I thought you said you'd done that before."

"I did." Teague got to his feet and began swiping off the wads of string from his clothes. "I got killed that time, too. Guess I should have learned my lesson, huh?"

"Some people just have a longer learning curve." She

flicked a speck of string from his collar. "Take me, for example."

"You?" He tucked his chin in and bent at the knees to bring them eye to eye. "You're one of the smartest people I know."

"Keep reminding me of that, will you? Because I may be about to do something really, really stupid." She bit her lip, brushed more debris off his shoulder, then lifted her gaze to his. "Or absolutely the wisest thing I've ever done."

"Wendie, do you mean...?"

"Just for the time the kids are at summer camp, I've decided I'll go with you on your publicity tour."

"You surely do look familiar, mister." Betty Jo Byerly, head tour guide for the Flying C, squinted at Teague through the cluster of campers' parents gathered in the lobby.

"Can't imagine why," he muttered, tugging his ball cap down until the brim touched his dark glasses.

Wendie tossed him an anxious look.

He took her hand and gave it a squeeze because he didn't dare flash a smile and risk exposure. They had agreed not to let anyone at the camp know who they were, not at this place, a ranch they now knew was sometimes mistaken for the Lost Romance Ranch of television fame. Not with the kids slated for a weeklong stay.

Betty Jo scowled. She tilted her white cowboy hat back, ruffling her short salt-and-pepper hair. Then she went on with the speech she'd obviously given so many times she could stop and start it without missing a beat.

"Once called the 66 Central Guest Ranch and Grill because of its proximity to the halfway mark of Route 66, the name changed to the Flying C Dude Ranch twenty-five years ago when the present owners took over."

Teague took mental notes as the woman went on.

"The I-40 bypass had already drawn the tourists away. As you probably know, this place ain't even really on 66, much less at the center, so it got even less travel."

Betty Jo held her hand out to point to a yellowed map. It only showed America west of the Mississippi. Still, it managed to cover half the wall in the cool, musty-smelling lobby of the main building.

Teague scanned the bold red line that jagged its way from Chicago to Los Angeles. Route 66. His pulse picked up just looking at it. When they left the twins here, that's where he and Wendie would be, on what Steinbeck had dubbed the Mother Road. Or on what was left of it.

"What they call the geomathematical center of Route 66 is over in Adrian, Texas." Betty Jo spoke without even seeming to connect with the words coming out of her mouth, as if she was totally unaware of what she was saying. She did seem, however, keenly aware of Teague.

He kept his head lowered.

She kept giving him quizzical, sidelong glances. "There is no more Route 66 in Texas beyond that point now, just as there are only bits and pieces of it between here and Amarillo. There are still some surviving landmarks, and the Flying C is proud to count itself among the must-see attractions still in daily operation from the former glory days."

Wendie leaned close to him and whispered, "Isn't this

place terrific? History, ambiance, acres and acres of wide-open prime Texas prairie, plus a dozen guest cabins. And you should see the stables!"

Behind his dark glasses Teague had the luxury of studying his wife's face without the awkwardness of being caught looking like an adoring idiot. He was an adoring idiot where Wendie was concerned, sometimes more idiotic than others, but he hated the thought of looking like one to a group of total strangers. He loved her and she loved—

He watched as she turned her face to the next map, a layout of the Flying C and its facilities.

She loved this ranch.

Betty Jo waved her hands about like a flight attendant going through the motions with her practiced speech. "The Flying C has been in continuous use as a dude ranch, for overnight accommodations, or providing quality summer youth programs since 1949. The exteriors of the buildings remain much as they were back then, but the interiors have had extensive updates and makeovers to keep them up to code and pleasant for our guests."

"It really is in great shape. It's even handicapped accessible." Wendie pointed to a sign on the rest room.

"Sounds like you've really done your research on this place," he whispered to his wife.

"Well, of course. I wouldn't send the kids to a camp if I hadn't done a lot of research on it first."

"Oh, so you just know all of this because of the camp?"

She tensed, folded her arms, then looked over her shoulder at him. "That and when I first got into town a real-estate agent showed me some places, and when I didn't find any I really liked, she told me this place might be coming up for sale soon, so..."

"All right then, parents, that concludes my part of the presentation. Your campers should have had time to stow their gear and should be just about ready for one more good-bye hug before you hit the trail." Betty Jo pointed in the direction of the cabins. "If there aren't any questions, I'll let you go now and look forward to seeing you in a week."

The group of adults began shuffling about, some moving closer to inspect the maps, some heading straightaway for the door. A few clustered around Betty Jo.

Someone asked about the food, another about the credentials of the camp counselors.

Wendie hesitated. She didn't seem ready to leave but didn't really have any reason to stay that Teague could see—unless, of course, she wanted to put off being alone with him for as long as possible. He stuffed his hands in his pockets. He'd hoped she'd share his excitement about this undertaking, for the travel, the adventure, and the chance to get to know one another all over again. But Wendie had acted anxious and unsure all morning, until they got to the ranch itself. Then she came alive with a new energy and anticipation, all for the ranch, not for the trip or seeing him again.

When he'd come to pick the family up this morning he had not seen them for five whole days. The camp schedule had been chosen long before his arrival, and he had had to go back to California to close up his house and check on things before the trip.

Much as he had wished he could just hang around with Wendie and the kids, he put his own wants aside for the sake of Wendie's desire for privacy. No way could he have stayed in Wendie's small town for that long without somebody noticing and making the connection.

He watched as Wendie inched closer to the group asking questions of the tour guide, and away from him.

A tall man at the back of the group asked, "Doesn't this place have some kind of legend that goes with it? You know, like an outlaw gang stayed here, or it was the set for a movie or something?"

Wendie stopped in her tracks.

"Yeah, didn't they base a TV show on this place, back in the eighties?" A woman near the front of the group looked to the others for confirmation of her memory.

"No, afraid not." Betty Jo shook her head. "Just a rumor. Neither the old 66 Central Guest Ranch and Grill nor the Flying C Dude Ranch was ever the model for the Lost Romance Ranch."

Wendie spun around so fast, Teague thought she might give herself whiplash.

Betty Jo's head jerked up so quick, he thought she ran the risk of suffering the same affliction. She spoke to the crowd, but her keen eyes were trained dead on him as she finished, sounding even more distracted than before. "Though if people thinking it was brings guests in for a week, a night, or even a meal, the present owners don't object to the association."

"Let's get out of here before she makes an association that I'll want to object to." Wendie snatched his hand as she hurried toward the door.

In a few seconds they were out the door in the blazing sunlight. Wendie motioned to the twins, who stood near an empty corral with a few other children. They grabbed fast but fierce good-bye hugs and kisses by the car, then drove away, with Wendie waving to the children until long after they were mere specks on the horizon.

And they were on their way.

Neither of them said a word for several agonizing minutes. Then, finally, Wendie put one hand over her eyes and let out a long sigh.

"Tell me," she said so quietly that he had to strain to make sure he heard her over the highway noise. "Tell me I have not just made the biggest mistake of my life."

He tried not to feel hurt by her reservations. But the ache that Wendie's words caused in him colored the tone of his voice when he gritted his teeth as he promised, "Sweetheart, I will do more than tell you that. I plan to spend this whole trip proving it to you."

Six

I'm right, and you know it. If you want to see the Cadillac Ranch, you have to head back toward Amarillo. Now put that map away."

Wendie rattled the open paper, looked from him to the road, then sighed and began refolding the map back into a neat rectangle.

"We're headed the right way."

Wendie traded the map for a pocket-size yellow book she had stuffed in the side of her purse. "The guidebook says we should be able to see it from I-40. I don't see it."

"Forget the guidebook. We're out here to create our own adventure, not follow the checklist experiences suggested in some cheapo guidebook." He snatched it away and tucked it in his shirt pocket. "Trust me, okay?"

"We're off to a good start then? On the right track?"

Teague couldn't help but read more into the questions than they seemed on the surface. She wanted reassurance. She wanted to know they'd done the right thing. She wanted to know whether this was the first step toward healing their marriage or the beginning of the end of everything they cherished. Well, welcome to the club, he wanted to tell her.

Instead he said, "We'll come up on it pretty soon. You'll see."

"When we're there why don't we put the top up on the car?" She narrowed her eyes and tipped her face skyward.

"It's not too windy for you, is it?" He raised his chin, reveling in the air whooshing past. He liked the way it whipped Wendie's beautiful long hair around her face, the way it made him feel young and vibrant and carefree again.

"No, not too windy, but it is really clouding up fast. We get some powerful sudden showers in the summer in Texas, you know.

"Aw, you're just borrowing trouble."

"I'm telling you, they come up out of nowhere and pour down rain in sheets."

"It's not raining now, is it?"

"Not here, it's not."

"Then let's enjoy what we have. It's a summer day and I'm cruisin' 66 in a red convertible with my best girl beside me. What could go wrong with that?"

"For starters, we're on I-40 and your best girl is going to be your worst nightmare if she gets rained on."

"Wendie?"

"Yeah?"

"Read your guidebook." He tossed it to her.

She laughed, then opened up the thin volume. "It says here the Cadillac Ranch was placed by Texas millionaire and art collector Stanley Marsh 3."

" 'Three'?"

"Well, that's how it's written." She showed him the

page as if he could actually see it as he sped down the highway.

"I'll take your word for it."

"Anyway, let's see, it says ten Cadillacs...different years...some with fins...placed in concrete...1974. Whew. Sorry for skimming, but reading in the car is not my forte."

"Then stick with what you do best."

"Okay, I'll go back to telling you that you need to put the top up on this car." She smiled at him, but her tone carried an undercurrent of annoyance.

"Nagging me is what you do best?"

"I like to think of it as looking out for you."

It was subtle, but he appreciated the difference.

"Those clouds do not look friendly, Teague."

"Ha! Relax, will you? What harm could a few little clouds do?"

Overhead a low, threatening roll of thunder resonated through the swiftly gathering clouds.

What could a few little clouds do? He regretted the words almost as soon as they left his lips, but even more so five minutes later. They'd missed Exit 62, the way to the famous row of Cadillacs sticking straight up out of the Texas prairie, noses in the dirt, fins in the air. That didn't help matters.

"Don't worry, we can go back and find the exit. We're not on a tight schedule today." He tried to sound cheerful and unfazed by the irritating mistake. "We don't have an appearance until tomorrow in Tucumcari."

"Weather permitting," she muttered.

He did not believe in omens, but if he did, the fact

that this eventful trip had already started on the wrong foot might just be one of them. "We've got the open road, plenty of time, and each other. What more could we want?"

"How about an umbrella?" Wendie tipped her head up and held one cupped palm open.

"Would you let that go? I'm telling you, it's not going to—" A cool, fat raindrop plopped right in Teague's eye. "Not to worry, I still have everything under control."

"I wasn't worried until you said *that*." Wendie pulled a face to show her mock panic.

At least she was being a good sport about it, he thought as he reached for the dashboard. "It's a fully automatic roof. At the slightest hint of rain, all I have to do is push a little button and..."

Lightning flashed. Thunder roared. The sky opened up to release a torrent of water on them. The car's roof did not move.

"Um, honey, this is as much of a 'hint of rain' as I can take." Wendie's bold gestures sent water flying. "Could you push the button?"

"I can't find it. That is, I can't see it, and I can't look for it and drive at the same time, not in this downpour!" He shouted to make himself heard over the slapping of rain on the windshield, the seats, his wife.

"Let me try!" She lunged forward.

The radio came on, blaring an updated version of "Stand by Your Man."

"At least it wasn't 'Raindrops Keep Falling on My Head.' " Wendie was not amused by his joke.

The radio snapped off.

Teague struggled to keep the car on the road with rain pelting him in the face all the while.

"Pull over," Wendie demanded.

"Don't think I should. Can't really see all that well. What if I don't get completely off the road? We could get hit."

"You can't see well enough to pull over, but you *can* see well enough to drive?"

She spoke in a deceptively quiet voice through clenched teeth, and he could almost see steam rising off her skin.

"Let me at that radio again. Maybe I can tune in the reality station for you." She pushed her hair from her eyes.

"Just let me try one more time to find the right button." Eyes fixed on the road, he made a blind stab at the dash.

"Why won't you listen to me? Just pull over."

"Fine, I'm pulling over." He eased the car to the side of the road until he felt gravel under the tire, then let it go a little farther, wanting to make sure he was off the highway.

"I'm going to get out and see if there's a way to manually put it up."

"Wendie, don't bother." Teague reached for the button he could now see plainly. "It just takes a—"

She flung open the passenger door. She swung her feet out. She slipped in the grass and went sliding down to the ground with a thud, landing with her legs sprawled out, her back straight as an arrow, and her behind in the mud.

On cue, the roof whirred into action, rose slowly against the gray-white sky of the waning storm and eased itself over the top of the rain-soaked convertible. The rain stopped.

Teague leapt out. He rushed around the car to find his wife sitting in the mud and gravel, her hair damp, red clay streaked on her face and clothes. "Wendie? Are you okay? Did you hurt anything?"

"Just my pride." She struggled to stand, but her feet started to slip out from under her.

Teague was there in a heartbeat. He lurched forward and caught her up close to his body, holding her firm to keep her safe. It felt good. It gave him hope for the trip and for the relationship he hoped to rebuild while on it.

Then she pulled away from him. "This is a total mess. I can't believe we haven't even seen our first landmark, and we've already had our first disaster."

"Hey, we got it out of the way fast. Now we can relax and enjoy the rest of the trip."

"Easy for you to say. You don't look like the victim of a low-budget mud bath."

"Would it help if I told you I think you look gorgeous?"

"It would help if we were not having this discussion by the side of the road." She shook her hands, slinging red mud onto the white car top and flicking tiny flecks of it onto her seat. "Oops. Sorry."

"It's just a car." He held his hand out. "Get in and I'll take you someplace where you can get cleaned up. There's a highway rest station not too far back in the direction we came from."

"The direction we came from is not the direction we're

going." She folded her arms, then cocked her head. "Is it?"

"You know, Wendie, the way this trip is starting out, I don't know whether we're coming or going. But the ranch is that way." He pointed. "And the rest stop is that way. You say I never listen to you or take your needs into account, so let me start here and now. Tell me what you need to do first, clean up or drive on, then take the hike to the Cadillac Ranch."

"We have to hike to it?"

"Just up a dirt path."

"Well, I can't get any dirtier than I am now—"

"Not and be allowed back in my car, you can't." He smiled.

She gave him a hard glare as she marched past and climbed into that very car. "Let's go and get it over with."

"I hear and I obey."

She slammed the door shut.

"Well, things have gotten off to a rousing start," he muttered as he came around to the driver's side. "In fact, if things keep on the way they've begun, we'll be divorced before we ever reach Santa Fe."

"I thought it would be...better somehow." Wendie squinted at the row of ten Cadillacs thrust upward from the dry dirt and covered with graffiti. "More shiny and, well, grander, I guess."

"There's not a lot of grandeur left on the remnants of Route 66 anymore, Wendie."

She lifted a small camera to one eye and squinted at

him with the other. The camera clicked as she took a couple of quick photos.

"That's part of the charm, I think," he said. "The simplicity, the human element versus the slick packaged techno-glitz of most of what we see today. No gleaming amusements, no hype, no pretense. It is what it is, and it connects us with what was."

"You sound like a philosopher."

He shrugged. "Guess this place brings it out in me."

"Like it does in a lot of people." She turned to look over some of the things scribbled, painted, even etched into the automobile bodies behind her.

"Read some of the notes people leave along with their names and initials—song lyrics, dates, slogans, memories." He walked toward where she stood in front of the line of cars.

"People have been doing this since 1978?"

"The cars have been repainted periodically, but yes, people have long wanted to leave a reminder of their presence, make some kind of mark on the Mother Road, the way it did on them, no doubt."

"You are becoming a philosopher." She put a conciliatory hand on his arm.

The sun had come back out, the day looked bright. Her clothes were still soggy, but in the heat it didn't feel all that bad. She was glad she hadn't made him drive her to a rest stop to change, then back here to see the landmark. She only wished now she'd been a bit nicer to him about the whole thing. There must have been something about the mix of mud and humiliation that brought out the grouch in her.

She leaned in to read a short note left on the fin of a once proud vehicle. "It seems kind of sad, though, doesn't it?"

"That I've become philosophical?" He grinned at her.

"No, that people, as you called it, 'make their mark' here only to have it painted over again."

"Oh, I don't know. It seems fitting to me. You look at the cars, outdated, forgotten. You look at the road, fading, crumbling, more myth than reality for the most part. And you look at the thoughts and words of a person—they're all fleeting, temporary at best."

"Too much of what people try to make last just doesn't," she whispered, wondering if he felt the tug of emotion about their own relationship in her words.

"Then you look out at the land and the seemingly endless expanse of sky here, and you can't help but think about what does last, what is permanent."

"God's creation, God's love, God's word."

He simply nodded.

She took his hand and they stood there a moment, neither saying a thing. Then they returned to the car, got in, and headed back for the interstate and away from the quiet monument to the old road. But Wendie knew they each took away a little piece of this place and what it stood for.

Teague guided the soggy-seated convertible into a rest stop. He'd even put the top back down in an effort to help dry things off.

Wendie shifted on top of the opened road map that was protecting the seat from her muddy shorts. Getting into the car again had only renewed her irritation with him. It had only reminded her how easily he ignored her feelings and how he did not want to listen to her even in small things. He could dry things off, she thought, but he couldn't cool them off. He could not cool off her anger toward him as they drove on, wet, dirty, and windblown.

"Looks like there's a nice-sized rest room where you can change and get cleaned up a bit." He pulled the car past a long chartered bus and into a space in front of the building. "Suppose we go to our neutral corners and promise to tackle this problem when we get back on the road, say in twenty minutes?"

Wasn't that so like Teague to think the hurts, the misunderstandings, the needs, the love and anger of all these years could be sorted out in thirty minutes? Or in a week on the road? Why had she come on this trip with so many impossible hopes—she peeled herself up from the seat—and with so few changes of clothing?

She didn't say another word to her husband as she dashed for the rest room. She held the suitcase he'd retrieved from the trunk strategically to cover her filthy backside. Alone inside, she quickly changed clothes, stuffed the damp outfit into a plastic bag, and repacked her suitcase. A quick glance in the mirror told her she needed to wipe some mud off her face and try to get a comb through her damp, tangled hair.

She clenched her teeth and let warm water gush into the white ceramic sink in front of her. If Teague had just listened to her in the first place, none of this ever would have happened. She thought he had changed, but had she hoped for too much?

She washed the dirt from her face then dove into her purse. The brush snagged through her hair and loosened a snarl or two but did not improve the overall look of the wind-whipped mess. She sighed and decided maybe just a touch of makeup would make her feel better.

As if anything on the surface could ease the conflicting emotions churning inside her at this moment. She slicked a pale gloss over her lips and recalled not just Teague's last kiss but every kiss they'd ever shared. She brushed dark mascara over the tips of her long lashes and remembered all the tears that had collected there. Not all had been for her broken heart. There had been tears of joy at her children's birth, and tears of laughter when her sides ached, and tears of pride at Teague's accomplishments, and misty-eyed moments when she realized how much he truly, fully loved her.

She sniffled. The emptiness of the tile room made it sound louder than she expected. Once more she questioned her own motives for being on this trip with Teague. For the past few days she had tried to convince herself that the twins' welfare was her primary concern. At the very least, they deserved to have parents who could learn to get along, to cooperate with each other. Of course, she was really hoping to provide her children with a whole family again. That would only happen if Teague could prove to her during these two weeks that he had indeed changed. He was off to a rotten start.

Wham!

Wendie jumped as a gaggle of teenaged girls came pouring into the rest room.

"Did you see him?" One high-pitched voice rose above the rest of the chattering crowd.

"See him? He spoke to me."

"That's nothing, he touched me!"

"He was just trying to get out of the door that you were blocking."

"Can you believe how cute he is?"

"Those eyes!"

"That smile!"

Wendie gave a secretive smile at the girls' obvious crush on some cute boy. They sounded just like the young fans of years ago who had idolized Teague. She'd been wildly jealous of them then, and why wouldn't she have been? No matter how much he let Wendie know he loved her, he did not often let the fans in on that fact. The fans, his career, his image came first. It was part of the job, he'd say. He could justify it all he wanted, but it never took the sting away.

"I still can't believe I got so close to him," a young lady with short, curly hair said dreamily.

The door swung open, and a new woman entered, speaking in an authoritative voice to the cluster of teens. "Hurry up, y'all. The bus leaves in fifteen minutes."

"Of course, none of us got as close to him as Miss Marshall did," a girl called out from the back of the room. Her remark was answered by hoots and laughter from the others.

"I was just being friendly." The new woman, apparently the infamous Miss Marshall, came to stand right next to Wendie at the row of sinks.

Wendie gave her a nod and a cursory glance.

She had brilliant red hair and porcelain skin and couldn't have been a day over twenty-five. Their gazes met in the mirror, and the woman smiled. "Nothing wrong with a girl being friendly now, is there?"

Suddenly Wendie's own reflection looked old and boring. She managed a smile. "It's always nice to be friendly, that's for sure."

"Yeah, right. There wasn't anything *nice* about your style of friendliness, Miss Marshall," a tall blonde teased. "I can't believe you walked right up to him and threw your arms around him!"

As fast as her hands could collect them, Wendie stuffed her things into her bag and snatched up her suitcase. She'd had a lousy day and having to hear this kind of conversation did nothing to improve it.

"You did that, Miss Marshall?"

Wendie pushed her way almost to the door but couldn't make her way through one last knot of girls. "Excuse me. Could you let me through?

"Miss Marshall! You actually threw yourself at Dash Logan?"

Girls squealed with laughter and delight.

Wendie froze. *Dash Logan?* She knew the name, but she wasn't quite sure…

"That's just his name on the soap opera," someone in the crowd informed them. "His real name is something even hotter—like Tiger or Tease."

Wendie's body went numb. The path to the door was unobstructed, but she could not make her feet move.

"It's Teague Blackwell. He's been a star since like my

mother was a little girl. He's still cute but not likely to care much about girls your age, y'all." Miss Marshall said it as though that excused her aggressive behavior. "That's why out of all of us crowding around to speak to him, I was the one he lavished his attention on."

Wendie had no right to feel betrayed by that, but she did.

A plain-looking young woman in glasses stepped through the crowd. "He only put his hand on your shoulder to fend you off, Megan."

"He did not have to fend me off, Judy, I assure you." Miss Marshall forced the words through clenched teeth.

"Megan, you are here not just to watch over these girls but to be a role model. Neither your tall tales nor your throwing yourself at that poor man sets a very fine example."

Miss Marshall glowered.

"He told her," the detractor began, drawing the focus onto herself, "that he didn't kiss fans or hug fans anymore. He said that even though he was on TV, he had the right to set boundaries, and more than that, he had the obligation to his lovely wife and he wouldn't do anything to put his most important relationship in jeopardy."

Wendie's heart leapt, and she sighed along with the dozen young romantics.

"She's the luckiest woman alive," one of them declared.

Unexpectedly Wendie blushed but quickly recovered when she saw that not a single eye was trained on her. She smiled and wondered how the girls, who were all now vying for a spot at the mirror, would react if they knew that she was the lucky woman in Teague's life.

"You think you're something, don't you?"

Wendie startled and looked to see who might have spoken to her. No one looked back.

She did see Miss Marshall corner Judy, who was obviously older than the teens but not by much, near the trash can. "You just said those things because Dash, or Teague, or whatever, was too busy admiring me to hear you ask for an autograph because you're such a fan of that stupid old ranch show he was on."

The pain flashing in Judy's eyes made Wendie feel she had to do something. With renewed wonder at hearing how Teague had put her first even though she wasn't there to see it, she hurried outside. When she saw Teague standing beside a bus, she made a beeline for him.

"Honey," he greeted her with a friendly nonchalance clearly intended to protect her identity.

She drew in her breath and set her suitcase down beside him.

"I'd like you to meet Mr. Tanner. His group is headed for a band competition."

She slipped under Teague's elbow and wrapped her arms around his trim waist, beaming a broad smile at him, then at Mr. Tanner, then back to Teague. "Nice to meet you. I already had the, uh, pleasure of encountering some of your group."

"What's with the hug?" Teague kept his voice low. "You're not secretly planning to squeeze the life out of me for the rain thing are you?"

"Can't a wife show a little affection—or a fan shower you with attention?"

Teague rolled his eyes heavenward and groaned.

"I'm sorry about that little incident," Mr. Tanner rushed to explain. "Our insurance doesn't cover parents riding the buses anymore, so we had to take teaching assistants to act as chaperones for the ride. Some of them are practically kids themselves, and when they saw Mr. Blackwell, well, they just got a little..."

"Friendly?" Wendie asked through a tight smile.

Teague squirmed.

He deserved that much for his stubborn refusal to put the car top up. She crooked her finger and beckoned him. "Can I see you alone for a minute, darling?"

"That insurance of yours, Mr. Tanner? You said it doesn't cover parents riding along, but do you think it would cover a husband stranded at a roadside rest stop? I may be in need of a ride..."

"Ha! You should be so lucky, pal." Wendie thrust her suitcase into his free hand, then tugged at his arm. "Come on, we have to talk."

He followed along until they were out of earshot, then finally dragged his feet to a stop. "If you don't mind, I think I'd rather stay where there are still some witnesses around."

"Very funny."

"So I assume you heard about that little girl making a pass at me?"

"There was nothing little about that girl, Teague."

"I tried to sidestep her," he continued without losing a beat for Wendie's sarcasm. "But before I knew it she had..."

"Say no more." Wendie's hand went up, her jaw winding tightly. More than ever she wanted to carry out her plan. "I got used to that kind of thing years ago—and when it comes right down to it, I no longer have the right to be upset by it."

Eyes darkened, Teague moved over her. His shoulders rose protectively. "That's not how I see it, Wendie. All your wifely rights are intact as far as I'm concerned."

Wendie raised her fingers to his lips. "As I was saying, I can't stop someone from throwing herself at you. I can, however, teach her a little something about being nice to people."

"What do you mean?"

A few minutes later, Wendie stole a peek at her husband as they stood on either side of Judy and waited for their picture to be taken. When that was done, Wendie turned to the girl, who was now a VIP to an entire busload of kids. She handed Judy the pen and pad of paper they had been using to sign dozens of autographs.

"Now, you write down your address, and I'll send you any memorabilia I can part with."

"Gee, Wendie, it's been so exciting to meet you. Claire was my favorite character on *The Lost Romance Ranch.*" The girl blushed and gave Teague a meek but adoring look. "Not that I didn't like Ryder."

Teague smiled. "And the idea of Claire and Ryder getting together?"

"It's perfect," the girl said, confirming what she and the others had told them moments before. "Though part of me just wishes they'd never do a reunion of the show, so I can imagine them always just as they were."

Wendie gave her husband a smirk. "Thanks, Judy. It was so nice to meet such a big fan."

Teague gave Judy a pat on the back as she boarded the already loaded bus. He waved good-bye and wished them well on their trip.

"Speaking of trips..." He gestured toward the car.

"We've still got a long way to go." Wendie gave him a sidelong glance.

"I understand that."

"Good."

"Let's hit the road, then. Route 66 awaits."

Seven

Teague drove on through the unremarkable flatland. Wendie hummed brightly along with an oldies radio station, and he began to relax. Though he thoroughly approved of Wendie's behavior back at the rest stop, he had no idea what had brought it on. It just wasn't like her.

When she had retired from acting after the birth of the twins, she had shut the door on everything that had gone with the business. She did not sign autographs. She never used her maiden name, the name that still ran on the credits on the reruns: Wendie Keith. Even when she had left him, she had remained Wendie Blackwell. That gesture had fired his resolve to win her back and given him hope that he could do just that.

He glanced over at his wife, her chin up, the sun on her closed eyes, the breeze lashing lightly through her hair. She took great pains to make sure she didn't look like the character of Claire she had played on television. That wasn't difficult since she'd played a rough-edged ranch girl with her hair always in braids, her clothes always in shambles, and her heart always in the right place. One of the reasons Teague had wanted to do the movie was to give Wendie a chance to shine, to step out of the shadows of that image and show everyone the woman that he saw.

She shifted in the seat. Her head lolled to one side.

He smiled at her, though he knew she did not notice it. He wanted the world to know how bright, funny, smart, and beautiful his Wendie was.

She'd shown a little bit of her true potential to her fans today when she'd posed with the sweet-natured Judy at the rest stop. But what had made her do it? Could he take that as a sign that she was warming to the spirit of the trip, to the movie idea, to him?

She sighed in her sleep.

He wanted to ask about her motivation. But he wondered if this was one of those "listening" things, one of those things she expected him to somehow instinctively know.

They'd only been traveling for a few hours and already had one disaster and one mystery under their belts. It was too soon to stir things up any more than that. He'd wait, watch, listen, and learn for a while longer before he opened up any serious discussions. Best to let sleeping dogs lie. Wendie, on the other hand...

"Hey, sleepyhead, wake up!"

"I wasn't sleeping; I was resting my eyes." She rubbed them with both hands.

"You're going to miss the Last Motel in Texas/First Motel in New Mexico that way."

She snatched up her guidebook. "Does that mean we're nearing Glenrio?" She flipped through the pages and squinted. "Let's see..."

"Um, actually—"

"According to this, Glenrio straddles the border of Texas and New Mexico, but there isn't much left of the place. Empty gas stations and a few houses. This says that motel and its famous sign aren't even around anymore."

"Most of the old road is just plain gone in these parts. The towns that used to depend on it just faded away."

"Ghost towns?" She feigned a shudder.

"Seems as good a description as any, ghost towns along a ghost road. Some places it just vanishes into gravel or into patches broken up by grass and weeds."

"Everything I've read says more is lost all the time, despite the work of preservationists."

"Yeah. It's sadder than I thought it would be to see the disrepair."

"Sounds like in some places there's no way of knowing we're anywhere near the old road without, oh, say, a *guidebook*."

He laughed. "Yet there is still a sense of what once stood here, the life and hope and energy that once filled these places."

"You sound like you're talking about the ruins of the Roman Empire," she teased.

"Maybe I am, in a way. Those ruins are the remnants of roads and civilization that rose and fell while ordinary people struggled to try to make things better. Route 66 is just the fading dream of a time too brief in history."

"It gets to you, this place, doesn't it?"

"Yes, it does." It and the company made him nostalgic, without a doubt.

He lifted his gaze over the unchanging flatland and

for an instant wondered if this was how it felt to be out on the open sea, this feeling of being totally alone except for God and immediate company. It was at once freeing and frightening to him.

"It does get to me. Not that I ever spent a lot of time here, but we did come out to a lot of these places to do publicity photo sessions and location shots for the show, remember?"

"Not me. You were the angel of Route 66. I was always back at the ranch." She flapped her elbows like a hayseed in a hoedown.

"Well, we've fixed that now. You're on the open road —or what's left of it—out to meet some of the people touched and entertained by our characters and our show."

"If the guidebook is right, we won't find many of those in Glenrio."

"Fans?"

"People."

He laughed. "Actually we're coming to Adrian next."

"Then why'd you wake me up to see the Last/First Motel?"

"I thought you said you weren't sleeping."

The radio station faded. Wendie fiddled with the dial, got only static, then turned it off. Her tennis shoe began to bounce against the dashboard where she had propped her feet.

"All right, I admit it. I'd drifted off to sleep. Now you have to confess something."

He gripped the steering wheel. "Like what?"

"The real reason you woke me up."

"That's easy." He let out a long sigh. "I missed you."

"Missed me?" She tucked her hair behind her ear. "I was right here all along."

"Yeah, well, sometimes someone can be right next to you and still not really *be* with you. Do you know what I mean?"

"Know it? I moved all the way to Texas because of it."

"*That's* how you felt about me, about us?"

She dropped her feet to the floor and twisted her upper body toward him. "Yes! I've only told you that a thousand times. Which only leads me to the other reason—"

"Whoa! Hold it right there, Wendie." He held up one hand while still maintaining control of the car with the other. "Before you go off on that tangent about me not listening, let me just say that I never heard that—that you missed me even when I was there. I heard I worked too much, put my career before you and the kids—"

"It's the same thing."

"It is not the same thing. My work habits, the way I show my love to you and the twins, those are all about me. All this time I've thought this was only about me, that if I just tried harder we could put our family back together."

"That's why we came on this trip, isn't it? To see how you've changed and if we can work things out."

"If we can work things out. But before now the only one working on anything has been me. What about you?"

"What about me?"

"What are you working on during this trip, Wendie?"

"Right now I'm working very hard at understanding what you're getting at." She smiled, but her eyes were wary.

"Well, you've obviously got some things you need to deal with, starting with the fact that you don't trust me."

"Trust? I never said that."

"Didn't you?" He had not wanted to get into such a deep discussion this soon into the trip, and yet he couldn't simply let it slide. "You said you walked out on me because even when I was next to you I wasn't really with you. That tells me that you don't have faith in me, that you don't fully trust my devotion to you."

She did not answer, and that was answer enough.

"You have hardened your heart toward me, Wendie, and nothing I do can alter that unless you are willing to change too."

"Me? Change?"

"You've just as much as told me that the things I thought I could do to save our marriage won't be enough. You have to do some of this work too. And the rest—well, I guess we'll have to leave that to God."

~

She set her jaw and stared out at the flat landscape whizzing by. The man made sense. When she looked deep into her own heart, she didn't trust him. That mistrust had fueled her every decision since he'd started sending her those gifts designed to pique her curiosity enough to watch him on that talk show. Up until he'd pointed out how her own hardness would keep them from mending their marriage, she had wanted to think all the blame for their problems rested with Teague.

Now she had to face the fact that she had as much work to do to save their relationship as he did. She had to rebuild her trust in her husband. She had to work to rediscover her faith in him and to learn to love him, fully love him again, the way she had vowed she always would.

And he had to do the same with her. She could no longer delude herself that this was simply a matter of his behaving differently. They had hurt each other, and they would both need the love of God and the patience of saints to deal with that in just one short week.

"This situation and the things you've said have given me a lot to think about," she said, folding her hands in her lap.

"Situation?"

"The trip. It creates a unique situation for a couple trying to figure out where to take their relationship, don't you think?"

"Too bad there's not a road map or a guidebook for that, huh?"

"Well, there *is* a guidebook."

"Yeah, I think I've heard of it. Bestseller, right?"

"And we both know what it would say on this subject."

In a single look he reminded her that she had been the one to go against the beliefs they both cherished when she had taken the children and moved away. She clenched her jaw and crossed her arms over the increasing tightness in her chest. "Of course, we have some other considerations that complicate matters over the next week."

"Talking about how difficult you're going to find it to keep from smothering me with kisses all the time now that we're alone together?"

"Not cute," she warned with a wag of her finger. "More remarks like that and the smothering part might begin to tempt me though." Secretly she appreciated his attempt to lighten the mood. "No, I'm talking about *professional* considerations."

"Professional considerations?"

"You invited me on this trip to explore the possibilities for Claire's character, for the reunion show, to poll the fans." Wendie examined her hands as she spoke. "This journey isn't just about us exploring our relationship, you know."

"I know. Does your concern over this, the way you acted back at the rest stop by signing autographs and letting everyone know you were in the show, mean you're seriously considering doing the reunion? Given that everything else works out between us, of course."

Without looking up, Wendie lifted her shoulders. "No."

Teague mouthed her response back at her but gave no other comment.

"Let's say I'm on a fact-finding mission. Whether or not I do the show would depend on a number of things."

"Would I be out of line to ask what things?"

Wendie squared her shoulders. "First, I want to see for myself that people really do still remember and care about the show as much as you say they do." She ticked the comments off on her fingers as she spoke, trying not to sound haughty. "Next, I want to see how people react to the concept of Claire and Ryder getting together."

He opened his mouth and poked his index finger into the air to interrupt her.

She glowered at him.

He pressed his lips shut and put both hands on the wheel.

"Finally, I need to find out if I can play the role—not just of Claire but of the celebrity."

"You did fine with those kids back at the rest stop, Wendie." Teague's praise was tinged with humor as he added, "I don't think you should overestimate the amount of fame this project will generate though."

"Compared to what I'm accustomed to, if a stranger waves at me in the mall I'll feel like a star." She smiled, then offered belatedly, "And thank you, but when I revealed my identity at that rest stop, it was to perk up the self-esteem of that nice young lady, not to be recognized."

"And to embarrass that overly friendly fan of mine?"

She tipped her nose in the air. "I couldn't care less about your adoring public. It was her behavior in general that I found offensive."

That's great, Wendie, she told herself. Now that she'd made that bold proclamation she couldn't very well ask him if that kind of thing happened often since he became a…what had the TV talk show host called him? A hunk? Mentally she added that to her list of reasons for being on the tour.

"Look, Wendie, as for that girl's behavior, I was completely taken aback by it. You know that even when I was something of a teen idol, that had been expressed mostly in fan mail. I never had been chased or mobbed. Except that one time..." He let his voice trail off, and a dopey look came over his face.

The big ham, trying to get her going by pretending to recall some star-struck fan or wayward moment of his youth. Well, it wasn't going to work. He could not make her jealous with an unfinished thought or a wistful look. She stole a sidelong glance to see if he'd given up the charade yet.

He sighed.

"Okay, I give. I have to know. What are you grinning about?"

He graced her with a high-beam smile and flashed her a telling wink. "I was just thinking about all those years when nobody knew I was alive. Now, after a few months' exposure on daytime TV, I'm a bona fide sex symbol."

"Somehow I think you're adjusting to it.

"Is that sarcasm I hear in your voice, Wendie? Or could it be jealousy?" He practically crowed the question.

"I'm not jealous," she snapped. "I'm just the teensiest bit cranky because I'm hungry." Wendie pushed her lower lip out and gazed longingly at the town of Adrian coming into view.

"Hungry?" His eyelids fluttered shut then opened again as his eyes rolled up and to the right.

He was probably checking the rearview mirror, Wendie decided. Of course that theory didn't explain his disgruntled mutterings.

"Hungry, she says. The woman can't admit to a simple, honest emotion. Instead she pretends to be famished." Teague lowered his right shoulder to lean in toward Wendie and asked in a deep, hushed voice, "Is *famished* right? I wouldn't want to accuse you of feeling anything other than exactly…"

"Find a place to get something for me to eat, please, or the next honest emotion I'll admit to is rage, pal. I'll use it to explain to the nice police officer why I grabbed the steering wheel and drove the pretty convertible into a ditch, leapt out, and started gnawing on some poor cow's ear in search of sustenance."

He laughed. "That I would buy tickets to see."

"Do us both a favor and buy me a burger instead, okay?"

"You got it. Next stop Adrian, Texas, and good eats. Will that make you happy?"

Happy? She wasn't sure she remembered the nuances of that particular emotion anymore. It had been too long since she'd allowed herself to even hope for it. She looked across the seat to the man who had once made her happier than she could ever have imagined and who played his part in most of her recent misery. She bit her lip.

"Wendie?"

"Let's just stop and eat for now." She cocked her head to look out the window. "We'll be back on the road right after that and on to the rest of the trip and whatever it may bring. We can work on happiness later."

"I hope we don't have to wait too long, Wendie," he said softly as he parked the car.

Me neither, she thought.

Eight

They ate their meal without any further philosophical or emotionally charged conversation. They'd talked mainly about the grease content of the food and tried to see if they could tell the locals from the travelers. That mood, of talking without saying anything, lingered as they got back on the road again forty minutes later. Before long they found themselves in Glenrio on the Texas–New Mexico border.

Still, Wendie wondered about the new sense of quietude between them. Had the drive gotten to them, or had they simply begun to settle into a more comfortable way with one another? They had been married for fifteen years, after all, and known each other a great deal longer than that. Perhaps the awkwardness of their recent separation and their strained new "togetherness" had subsided enough. Now they could allow themselves the luxury of not having to fill up every silence with chatter. Or maybe they were both too wary of sensitive issues and old hurts to speak of anything more significant than the weather and what landmarks lay ahead.

She didn't know. She couldn't decide. She wasn't

even sure she had the ability to think about it objectively anymore.

"You want to pick one side or the other now?" Teague lifted his head up from the camera's lens.

"Hmm?"

"I've got a picture of you standing with one foot in each state, and this nice lady has offered to get one of both of us. I thought we'd stand on either side of the state lines."

"You in one state, me in another?"

"Kind of symbolic, don't you think?" He grinned at her. "Us standing side by side and yet in entirely different places?"

"Oh, uh-huh." *Too symbolic,* she thought, her heart sinking as he handed his camera to a woman with blue-gray hair and a straw handbag with bright flowers all over it.

"Do you want to stand in Texas or New Mexico?" He pointed to two identical scraps of ground, except for the fact that they were divided by an invisible, man-made line.

"I, uh..." She did not want such a picture. She did not want to have it haunting her the rest of her life, especially if things did not work out between them. "We've already got the requisite cornball state-line picture. Let's do something else."

"Like what?" He reached her side.

She looked around for some other photo op. Nothing inspiring presented itself. "This place is so...it's just almost not even a place anymore."

"Well, the old road was like its lifeline. Now the interstate is that main artery."

She raised her hand to shade her eyes. "Those trees sound alive. What is that?"

"Cicada. It's a bug." He held his fingers apart to indicate a fair-sized insect.

Wendie winced.

He laughed, his green eyes flashing mischief. He edged up on her casually. A little too casually for her comfort, and she tensed.

"Sometimes people call them locusts," he whispered in her ear.

"Eeeuw." She grimaced. "Maybe we should just do without a picture."

"What's-a-matter, Wendie? You're not afraid of a little..."

Something tickled the back of her neck. She squealed. Her feet scuffed up a cloud of red dirt as she skittered away. Her toe caught on a rock and she lurched forward. Her hands shot out in front of her to break the fall.

Teague lunged to catch her.

She clutched at him.

He wrapped his strong arms around her, making her feel safe and secure like nothing else could.

Just then the camera flashed and the older woman announced, "Ooh, that'll be a nice one. Real cute of both of you."

"Wonderful," Wendie called through a strained smile. "Thank you."

The woman set the camera with the rest of their things and gave a brisk wave. "No problem. Enjoy the rest of your trip."

"We will." Wendie waved and then said to him, "But

only if I can keep any creepy-crawly things at bay."

"It was just me tickling your neck, Wendie."

"I know."

"You should have seen your face. And the way you jumped! Straight up, two feet, I reckon." His broad chest moved against her back while his infectious laughter went through her in warm waves. "You sure have gotten jumpy in your old age."

She glanced over her shoulder at him. She struggled not to smile, not to savor the sweetness of his arms around her. "I am *not* old, but that trick sure is."

"Hey, you fell for it."

She could fall for a lot more than a silly prank if she didn't put some distance between them. She slipped out of his embrace. "Let's get back on the road. Like the signs say: Tucumcari Tonight."

He was not usually sentimental or reflective, but something in the company and the landscape brought it out in him. The narrow strip of remaining road that snaked along the open countryside was the stuff of legend. The Okies immortalized by Steinbeck in *The Grapes of Wrath* had used this road seeking refuge from the Dust Bowl of the 1930s. The road had been pitted and dangerous then, and age and decay had not improved it.

They'd had to leave Route 66 for a while, taking the sleek, silent interstate until they approached Tucumcari. Gliding back onto the old road again felt like a homecoming of sorts. It filled him with a sense of belonging.

Belonging was something he'd missed these last three months, and he welcomed even the hint of it. For a man longing to find his place in the world, and in the lives of his wife and family, these serene surroundings spoke to his spirit and imagination.

"Is it much farther now?" Wendie squirmed in the seat next to his.

"Getting restless already?"

"I had no idea how taxing I'd find just sitting and riding." She tugged at the strap of her seat belt.

"If ever you feel like driving on this trip, just holler."

"That might help. Then again, maybe it has nothing to do with the drive and more to do with the setting."

"You don't like it?"

"Oh, it's beautiful. It's awesome." She lifted her face as if soaking it all in. "The kind of awesomeness that leaves you unaware of trivial things like time and petty annoyances."

"I'd ask what petty annoyances, but I'm not sure I want to hear the answer."

She shut her eyes, then opened them again and went on. "It's the scale of things out here. On top of that, we drive and drive and never see another human being. It creates the feeling that we've been on this road a very long time. Do you know what I mean?"

"Yes. I think it might be like what a sailor feels when he's gone for days without seeing land."

"That's a good way to put it. It's breathtaking, but a little scary. I'm glad you brought me this way, and glad you're with me out here."

It wasn't some deep profession of undying love, but

it certainly lightened Teague's heavy heart. "It's good to share this with you, Wendie."

"But I'll still be happy to see the next town on the horizon."

"Tucumcari, the town of two thousand rooms."

"As long as it has two, I'll be a happy gal."

"I'm really sorry we can't stay at the Blue Swallow." Teague pulled her luggage from the trunk.

"I read about it in the guidebook. Sounds like a real favorite of the old landmarks." She took the makeup bag from his hand. "Pink adobe cottages with a glowing blue swallow lighting the night sky."

"A classic for sure."

"Have you seen the names of the motels around here?" Wendie, her overnight case in one hand, flipped open her guidebook with the other. "The Paradise, Royal Palacio, Safari, Cactus, Buckaroo, Sahara Sands, Aruba, Pony Soldier, Lasso, and Apache. Not to mention the Palomino, complete with an electric sign of a rearing horse and the words 'Whoa Palomino.'"

"We'll do a driving tour of the town later and see what's still to be found. For now, let's just unpack and freshen up."

"I'm all for that." She wiped her forehead with the back of her hand.

"It's not the Blue Swallow, but this place will have to do for the night and tomorrow night. I'm right next door, and the ice and vending machines are just around the corner." He took the room key and unlocked her door. He pushed it open with his shoulder, then leaned in to check it out before standing back to let her in. "It's not too shabby, is it?"

She stepped over the threshold. Stale air and dim light greeted her. She flipped the light switch, though that didn't brighten things much. The dark green carpet and drapes and harvest gold bedspread seemed to absorb the yellow glow of the single overhead bulb.

"Wendie?"

"Well, at the risk of sounding a bit like a snob…" She gently dropped her overnight case to the floor. "It's not exactly what I imagined they'd give the star of their promotional event."

"Wendie, I am not a star of this event—or anything." He placed his hand under her chin and edged it upward.

Even in the muted light she could see the depth of sincerity in his intense green gaze.

"I'm a draw. A name enough folks remember from the old show, or have heard of from the soap opera, to bring in the curious and the autograph seekers. And that's okay with me. I don't do this for the fame or any of that. I understand that's all fleeting and irrelevant compared to what really matters in life."

"I wish I could believe you, Teague." She pulled her face away from his touch and slouched down on the edge of the bed, rumpling the thin quilted spread. "Or I wish I could make you understand that's not how it felt to me when you put pursuing your career first and foremost in your life."

"I placed a high priority on providing for my family."

He remained in the doorway. "There's a difference."

"You could have provided for us in other ways that didn't take so much of you away from us," she said softly, not as an accusation but more a straightforward, pain-filled reminder.

"Acting and the business is what I know how to do, and I do it well."

She could not argue with that.

"I always had work, even if it wasn't star-quality, career-making work, Wendie. It paid the bills, gave us a nice life-style, allowed you to homeschool the kids, even made it possible for you to move away and keep a separate household with your own accounts."

She wadded the bedcover in her fist and dropped her gaze.

Teague shifted his weight. "I wanted us to have those things, well, most of them, as much as you did. But I have no idea how I would have provided them—or ever would—without the one kind of work I know I can do well."

She swallowed hard, unsure what to say to that.

"If you buy that ranch in Texas, you will have done it mostly with money I earned acting."

She angled her chin up, but her lower lip quivered. "If I do this reunion show, that money could go toward my buying the ranch."

"Don't make this about your money and my money, please. That's not how I meant it, and you know it."

She let her gaze drop to her hands folded in her lap. She shamed herself by reducing this complex issue to a petty yours-versus-mine one-upmanship. "I know."

"Good."

She smoothed her palm over the bedspread. She swept her gaze over the small room with its bolted-down TV and pictures of sailboats on the walls. Then, desperate for something to say, she smiled at him brightly. "Hey, it just occurred to me that my wanting that ranch might be one valid reason for doing this show. I'd think the hustler in you would pounce on that and start using it to your advantage."

"I don't want you to do this because I wrangled you into it or because you feel you have no other choice. I want you to do it because you want to do it." He braced his arm against the doorframe. "That's what I hope promotional events like this one tomorrow will accomplish."

Relieved to have a less personal topic to focus on, she pushed up from the bed and walked to the air-conditioner unit. With a flick of her wrist she switched on the fan. It clunked and coughed, then started up with a whine.

Teague's gaze followed her.

"It's not a bad room, really. It's clean, and judging by the way this thing is blasting out frosty air, it will cool down nicely. Why don't you come in and tell me more about the event tomorrow?"

"Most of this tour was thrown together on the fly, bookstores where David has already arranged signings, appearances to raise money for a library, nothing we need to do any planning or rehearsing for." He held up his hands apologetically. "Tomorrow we're doing something with an oldies radio station that has a live remote in town."

"Sounds fun. What about tonight?"

"Nothing on the schedule that I know of, but when I checked in, the clerk did hand me a message to call my agent."

"Okay, well, then maybe you'd better go."

"Yeah. I'd better."

"Got to make that call. Might be important."

"Probably not, but if it is, I'll let you know right a—wait a minute." For the first time he stepped fully into the room. "Maybe I should make the call from right here, if you don't mind."

"Of course I don't mind, but I'm not sure why..."

"Self-defense."

"I thought the martial arts were self-defense. You're not planning on fending off would-be attackers with a dial tone to the kneecap are you?"

"I plan to fend off any idea you have that I'm doing something behind your back."

Teague chuckled as he dialed.

Feeling awkward about listening in and yet knowing that's why he wanted her here, she pretended to unpack, though really she was just shuffling things around in her suitcase. "Talking to your agent is hardly doing something behind my back."

He cradled the receiver between his broad shoulder and jaw, and carried the instrument in one hand over to the lone chair. He sat down and looked at her, seeming to be both listening intently and concentrating wholly on their conversation. "You're the one who thinks I make plans to suit my needs, never taking yours into account, right?"

"Guess you did listen to that much."

"If I take this call in my room, alone, and make any decisions regarding us, the deal, or the tour, you could easily accuse me of that very thing."

She wanted to defend herself against that portrayal, but how could she? He was right.

"This is Teague. What's up?" Oblivious to her, he was focused on the news from his agent.

She studied him and shook her head. The picture he made, black hair glistening in the spotlight of the hotel lamp, hands gesturing gracefully to his unseeing audience on the other end of the line, told Wendie that this man would always be, first and foremost, an actor.

"Yes. I see. And?" Teague's deep voice created a drowsy hum in the background of her thought.

Despite his best intentions to take the call here in order to include her, she might as well have vanished from the quiet room.

He threw himself into the conversation.

She didn't dare speculate what the two were plotting, but every minute they stayed on the line without updating her fueled her anxiety.

"Okay, got that. Then what did you tell them?"

She stole a peek at herself in the mirror to insure her irritation was clearly readable and gasped. Instinctively her fingers went to her hair, fluffing here, smoothing there, but it was a lost cause. The hours of traveling had left their mark—and her beleaguered attitude wasn't enhancing her appearance one bit.

"And you gave them my response in no uncertain terms, right?"

His response? What about her response? He hadn't

even bothered to ask her, or at least tell her what he had responded to.

"You know we decided this from the very first. I'm not going to budge on that point at all."

Didn't that sound just like the man? The man she'd left in California because of that very attitude? She sighed. What she really needed was a long, hot shower. And her comfy pajamas. And dinner.

Teague's hollow laughter rang out behind her.

"Alone," she grumbled through clenched teeth. Why had she thought anything would change with him? This call did not represent a change of attitude but more a shift in behavior. He was simply acting the part he thought she wanted to see.

Teague kicked his legs up and placed his feet on the bed—her bed.

She scowled, but he didn't notice.

"You know, I've been thinking maybe we should bring in some fresh blood for some revisions. The more I look over this script, the more dated it seems."

Him? She was the one who pointed out that flaw! She felt heat rush to her cheeks despite the frigid air churning into the room from the console beneath the window. She had to get away before she said or did something she would regret. Snatching up her overnight case, she bolted to the bathroom.

"Wendie? What's the matter?" He covered the mouthpiece with one hand and shouted after her as she marched into the tiny bathroom. "I didn't commit you to anything. I'm being very careful not to even associate you with the script or project. That is what you wanted, right?"

She slammed the door in response.

He thought of hanging up and going over to see if he could get her to tell him what had angered her so, but just then the sound of the shower spray made him stay put. Let her cool off. The voice on the other end of the line demanded his attention.

"Teague? You listening? You still there?"

"Yes, sure, I'm here."

"Well, I'm going to need more than your feeling that the script is a bit dated to talk anyone into okaying a rewrite, you know."

"I know."

"You haven't forgotten that we have to get Wendie to agree to the reunion project before anything more can go forward with it, have you?"

"No. How could I? But things have gotten…complicated."

"Complicated how? From a personal or professional standpoint?"

"In this case, one affects the other."

"I don't like the sound of that. Of course, if personal complications mean things are on the mend with you two, no reason why you can't use that to sway things to your advantage."

Teague sat up. Wendie had made a joke suggesting much the same thing, that he used any opportunity to press his advantage. Now, hearing it from his agent, it twisted like a knife low in his gut. "I have no intention of using Wendie, in any way. I would think you'd know that about me."

"I didn't mean it as a bad thing, really. It's just that, well, when you want something, my friend, you don't let much of anything or anyone stand in the way of your getting it."

"You make me hope I never meet myself in a dark alley." Teague huffed. "Am I really that obnoxious?"

"Obnoxious? Who said obnoxious? Certainly not me." His agent gave a husky laugh. "*Persistent,* that's a better word for it. Persistent and charming. You get your way and usually end up convincing everyone else involved that this is their way, too."

"I do that?"

"It's not a bad thing."

"Maybe not in business. But in a marriage..." He ran one hand back through his hair.

"I don't know about marriage. That kind of advice you're going to have to get elsewhere. But on business, I'm your man."

"Okay, on business then." He sighed. He welcomed the change, but he wasn't sure whether he was reacting to his agent's exaggerating a character quirk or afraid the man might be right. "Our business is currently to help me make this project viable. How does that look?"

"How does it look? He asks me, how does it look? It looks half-baked, my friend. Without Wendie to play Claire to your Ryder, we got diddly. We got less than diddly. We got no interest whatsoever from the backers. They are already talking about other projects."

Teague dug his fingers into the taut muscles over his burning stomach. This was very bad news. Still, his agent had been known to overstate. "Are you sure about that? What about the idea of getting another actress to play Claire? With the rest of the cast committed..."

"Diddly," he enunciated carefully. "Who wants to see a reunion without the real Claire? It's like Skipper without Gilligan, Wilbur without Mr. Ed, the Bradys without the Bunch. You get the picture."

"I get it. No Wendie, no show." He looked up and caught a glimpse of his own reflection in the mirror. Who was the man he saw staring back? Was he the decent guy who put everything on the line for the sake of the people he loved, or was he the man who found a way to get whatever he wanted, even if it meant hurting others and lying to himself? He had to find out, and this trip was his best and last opportunity to do so.

"You got that right, and you'd better not forget it. No Wendie, no show."

"Then no show, no big deal."

"What? What are you saying? Where are your priorities, man?"

"In the right place, for once. In the right place. Whether we make this movie is not nearly as important to me as whether I am the man my family needs me to be. I'll keep you posted on both, pal."

Nine

"Teague Blackwell, get your adorable self in here and show me how you want this done!"

"Hold your horses, woman. I've got a few hang-ups of my own going here."

Wendie stuck her tongue out at her blurred reflection in the hand-rubbed shine on Teague's black cowboy boots. Filled with pride in her work, she inhaled the richly masculine scent of leather and shoe polish. She quietly whistled as she stabbed her soft cloth along the stitching to dab away any excess color.

She and Teague had reached an uneasy peace last night as he had explained why he took credit for her idea of updating the script. What he said made sense, but she was still not ready to trust his words. Her anxiety over his call to his agent yesterday proved that readily enough.

Today she would have plenty of time to watch the man as he put his intentions in action. The book signing would draw locals and tourists, fans of Route 66 and of Teague Blackwell. And for the first time in years, she would be part of it, sitting alongside as he interacted with them. This would be an important test of his resolve not to put his own desires first.

She rubbed at the toe of the boot to work away a dull smudge. Maybe it was just the habit of fifteen years, but she wanted him to look his best for the event. Maybe the busywork also kept her from worrying about what the day would bring. In less than an hour, she would step with her husband into the old spotlight. Small-time as it was, everything she hoped for and struggled against could well hang in the balance. "Amazing."

Teague emerged from the bathroom fussing with the ornamental bolo tie accenting his gray-and-white western shirt. "Thank you. I am rather amazing, aren't I? Didn't think I could still look this good, did you?"

"You clean up okay." She handed him his boots, stealing a peek from beneath her lashes at her handsome husband. "The 'amazing' wasn't about you, though, just a... personal observation."

"Well, it fits."

"What?"

"You." He held his hands out as he always did to silently coax her into a big hug. "Your personal observation fits you. You do look amazing."

"Do you like it? Really?" Wendie leapt to her feet but did not go to him. Instead, she twirled around, setting her flared denim skirt flouncing. "It's not too corny?"

"It's perfect, just like the lady wearing it." He let his arms fall to his sides.

"Thank you," she whispered, feeling anything but perfect for having rejected his peace offering. What harm would one quick hug have done?

"You're welcome." He nodded.

Uneasiness began to fill the air between them.

She flicked her hand over her skirt.

Teague sat to put on his boots.

Neither of them said a word.

Wendie wanted to say something. Then again, maybe she didn't.

Absently, Teague grappled with his string tie.

"What are you trying to do, hang yourself?" Wendie wound her delicate fingers around the heavy turquoise slide at Teague's throat, loosening the velvety braided-leather string. "Or were you just trying to make your face a complementary shade of beet red?"

He looked down into her face, smiled a distant smile, and patted her on the shoulder. "I guess I was just preoccupied."

"Nervous about the signing?" she ventured, knowing that couldn't possibly be it.

"Yeah. That's as good an excuse as any." He turned from her to snatch his Stetson from atop the TV and settle it on his head.

She turned away from him for one last primping session in the mirror.

His emerald eyes fastened on her reflection.

She wished she knew what to say to tell him how anxious she felt about all this without making him feel she was nagging.

Teague flashed his star-quality smile. "What do you think? Is the hat too much?"

She blinked at the image he made, so much like the young man she had first known so many years ago. "It's just like the one you wore in the show."

"The one in the show was a little more beat-up than

this one. Remember, I was kind of a poor man's angel."

She reached up and adjusted the brim so it shaded his eyes and gave him a mysterious stranger quality she knew the fans would appreciate. "Poor men might just be the ones who need angels the most."

"Poor men and poor fools. Do you suppose that means I have an army of them on my shoulders?"

"I believe in angels—though not like the kind you played on TV—and I believe you may just have one watching over you, but not because you're a fool or a poor man. You aren't either one of those."

"I must be, or I'd still have you and the twins," he murmured.

"Teague, this is hardly the time to start that discussion."

"I know. I apologize. I was just feeling nostalgic, dressed like this, seeing you like that."

"I'm sorry if..."

"No need for that. It's okay. For now we have a job to do. The show must go on." He drew a deep breath, and the concern that had clouded his features moments before seemed to fade away.

"Okay." She matched Teague's defensive life-as-usual routine with a dazzling grin. As they left the room, Wendie vowed they would have to find a way to work on their problems without inflicting any more pain on each other.

~

It was as close to a perfect day as any man with a good marriage gone awry could ask for.

The signing had been set up for midafternoon on the

stage, which was really the back of a flatbed truck. Later that evening it would hold a reunited band from the early sixties. The event organizer told Teague and the man he'd written the foreword for, David Penn, that they hoped to have a brief question-and-answer period before the signing.

They'd done the whole event up right, with a farmers' market, some crafts booths, and a few booths with games raising funds for churches and charities. The weather had cooperated, the sun shining but not scorching, the breeze stiff but not staunch. The crowd had been small at first. But by noon a nice cross section of people had gathered from the area, curious passersby and the expected fans of Route 66 and *The Lost Romance Ranch.*

Wendie looked back over her shoulder at him as they walked through the crowd.

He paused to sign an autograph and to remind the asker to buy a book.

Wendie walked on ahead.

He hurried to catch up with her. While he tried to remain cordial to people who recognized him, he couldn't help but think of them as intruders on his time with his wife. He'd never felt that way before. He didn't like it. It made him wonder if this was how Wendie felt, as if her life and marriage were being tromped on when people sought him out and he stopped everything to sign autographs and chat with strangers.

He found himself taking his wife's arm protectively and walking close to her as they wandered through the crowd.

"Excuse me, but are you Ryder Blackwell?" A woman with big sunglasses and graying hair snatched at his sleeve.

"I'm *Teague* Blackwell," he corrected her.

"That's right," she said, as if he needed her confirmation of who he was. "When did you get out of jail?"

Wendie turned toward them.

"I wasn't in jail. Now if you'll excuse us..."

"You certainly were!" The woman looked indignant that he suggested otherwise.

His wife shot him a look that said she was enjoying this.

"I can see why you might not want to talk about it, but surely you put that part in your tell-all book."

"I didn't write a book, just the foreword for a book on the legends of Route 66. I've never 'told it all' to anyone but my wife." He gave Wendie's arm a squeeze so as not to call too much attention to her. "And I've never, ever been to jail."

"You sure?" She scrunched up her face.

"Yes, pretty much. But thank you for recognizing me." He moved to make a getaway.

"Oh, it must have been one of them drug rehab places you were in. That's it."

If she hadn't shouted it, he would have kept right on walking, but some things had to be nipped in the bud before they got out of hand.

"Handle it," Wendie whispered. "However long it takes, I'll wait for you."

"Spare me the jailhouse-sweetheart jokes," he warned with a laugh. Then he pivoted to find the woman with all the misinformation just a few feet away.

"Prescription medicine?" She gave him an exaggerated wink. "That's what they always blame it on, back pills or pain relievers, what have you."

"My back is fine, and the only pills I take are aspirin." He good-naturedly refrained from adding he'd like a bottle of those right now.

"Oh, please. I read all about your problems in a magazine."

"Ma'am, whatever you read, it wasn't about me, I assure you."

"Yes, it was," she insisted. "I read all about how the kid from *West Road* was arrested for possession of cocaine and went to jail or to rehab or something like all them spoiled Hollywood stars and—"

"I starred in *The Lost Romance Ranch.*"

"Are you sure?"

Teague managed to laugh at that, but just barely. "I'm pretty sure."

He turned away from the woman and started back toward Wendie. The woman tapped him on the shoulder again.

"You sued your mother." Her tone was accusatory.

He wondered if there was such a thing as taking the 'considerate celebrity' bit too far. "We had some differences years ago that made the paper, but I never—"

"I knew it! All you child stars grow up to be nothing but trouble. It's all the stress they put you under, you know. Who wouldn't have problems having all that fame and money so young only to lose it?"

"Actually, I have a great deal more money now than I did then, ma'am. And as for having lost my fame, that simply isn't true."

"Oh? You think so?" She tipped her nose up haughtily.

"Apparently not. Out of all the people in this place

today, you recognized me, even going so far as to recall personal details of my life."

She scowled but did not interrupt.

"In contrast I haven't the slightest idea who you are, and—while I'm sure you are a lovely person—that suits me just fine." He tipped his head to say good-bye, then quickly took Wendie by the arm and hurried away.

"In all the time I've known you, I have never seen you treat a fan like that." Wendie poked him with her elbow, but her smile told him she did not disapprove of his actions all that much.

"She wasn't a fan, Wendie, she was..." He looked down into her eyes. "She was an imposition. Certainly not my first priority, even in a promotional situation like this."

The rest of the afternoon he tried to keep his focus on his wife, on her needs and what he could do to make her happy. To his surprise it wasn't as difficult a task as he suspected it might be. The more concessions he made for her sake, the less she seemed to expect.

She made lively conversation with real fans and answered questions about the show and the actors who had worked on it. She seemed relaxed in the old role of celebrity and yet always had a look of relief when, if someone got too personal or assertive, he stepped in to draw the line between the professional and the private.

Though the other fans they met treated them both with more kindness and respect than the first woman, with each recognition one point was hammered home to him—he was loved. *Loved.* Emphasis on the past tense. No one asked what he was currently doing, and only a few asked what he was planning. It seemed pretty well a consensus that as an actor he was a relic.

Perhaps he should have felt past his prime. Yet somehow he suddenly felt like a man just coming into his own. Like some cliché, he could actually sense the closing of one door in his life and the opening of another. He did not need the adulation of strangers to reassure him that he would always have work, always be able to provide for his family.

It gave him some peace to know he really was a changed man, regardless of how Wendie would eventually choose to perceive him. And it felt right that he had changed of his own volition, out of his need, rather than to please a woman, no matter how much he loved her. This change was probably a long time coming, and this trip and Wendie's ultimatum only forced him to make the last step in a long process.

Still, winning Wendie's affection for keeps was no small prize. The love of his wife and family were more precious to him than any adoring fan or the promise of a future filled with scripts and opportunities. He understood that now, and he could only hope he knew how to transform it into something that Wendie could believe in again.

Wendie climbed the stairs leading to the flatbed stage, aware of the narrow passage and the precarious steps. She felt Teague's steadying hand on her back to guide her.

David Penn, the author of the book they'd come to

promote, led the way. He took the lone chair to the left of the podium and left the other two chairs for her and Teague. All three of them quickly settled in, their faces set in broad smiles and their eyes narrowed against the glare of the afternoon sun.

Since people had come to see him, Teague had politely removed his hat for the question-and-answer period and signing. Wendie felt more than a little tempted to snatch it up and push it down low on her own head, then slink off into the crowd incognito. Or as incognito as a woman fleeing a stage wearing an oversize cowboy hat could get. She left the hat where Teague had placed it and took a deep breath.

The prospect of becoming a public persona again, even to this small, enthusiastic crowd, had the butterflies in her stomach doing loops and tailspins. All day long, whenever the questions and constant strain of having to "sparkle" for the fans had overwhelmed her, Teague had intervened with his quick wit and easy charm. Aside from the first woman they'd encountered, he never had so much as a sour look for any of them. Yet for the first time in a very long time, he had not done this at the expense of Wendie's feelings.

She sat straight in her chair and scooted it back just enough so that she could watch the man without being obvious about it.

He waved to the gathering and pointed to people they'd conversed with earlier. From the moment he stepped on stage he had become the focal point. His smile alone set several women giggling and sighing.

How many of the women around her would gladly

trade situations, casting aside their treasured, uneventful lives for what they presumed she had? Wendie watched their doting expressions. She felt many would consider it. But when she saw the men beside them, holding their hands, whispering to them, sharing a laugh, when she saw the children standing in front of them or balanced on their hips, she revised her assessment.

If Teague's chosen lifestyle threatened their children's happiness, each and every one of these women would do as she had. Any of them would choose to maintain normality for their children over life with an unpredictable actor. Wouldn't they? She'd done the right thing then, and if he could not show that he had truly changed, she would do the right thing again.

But maybe she was worrying for nothing. What if Teague was a new man? He certainly seemed different, but how could she be sure?

Wendie squirmed in her seat, feeling a little ashamed. That attitude certainly wasn't one of open-mindedness toward Teague or his project. She promised herself to make more of an effort to consider doing the show, no matter how distasteful the prospect was to her.

That very topic surfaced when she swung her attention back to the question-and-answer session. Teague had all but taken control of the stage, but David and the host didn't seem to mind as they sat intently listening to some amusing story.

A round of applause signaled its end, and the moderator pointed to a young man in the front row.

"I grew up watching *The Lost Romance Ranch.* It was my mom's favorite show."

Teague gave her a doesn't-that-make-you-feel-old look over his shoulder, then turned to the fan and said, "Well, it was a top-rated family show for a long time."

"Yeah, well, I read somewhere that they're thinking of doing one of those reunion shows of it? Is that true, and when would it be on TV?"

Teague looked at her again, but his expression had lost all its playfulness. He paused for effect before speaking. "That project is currently on hold, I'm afraid."

The crowd gave a collective groan.

Wendie gasped and sat forward in her seat.

Teague shrugged. "Frankly, we're having some second thoughts about it. After all, we don't have anything new or important to say with a movie like that. Maybe it's best to let Ryder, Claire, and the gang live on in people's fond memories instead of bringing them out for an encore that might not be all that satisfactory—to either the actors or the fans."

"Not do a reunion show? Are you kidding?" The moderator put his hands on his hips, scowled at Teague, then swung his gaze toward the audience. "What do you all have to say about that?"

The group gave a murmur of discontent.

"Wouldn't you love to see how the characters' lives turned out?"

"Yeah! Absolutely," and other affirmations rose from the audience.

"Am I the only one who ever wonders if Ryder earned his wings? If he and Claire ever got together?"

"No!"

Wendie blinked.

To his credit, Teague did not gloat.

All around her, voices began to cheer the moderator's sentiments. For one moment, happiness at Teague's willingness not to do a reunion movie clashed with excitement over the crowd's outpouring of support for the project. As she regained her control, snatches of the audience's comments found their way into her thoughts.

"When I was a kid, I was a nerd like Claire. That character made me take pride in being a smart girl."

"I knew that the stuff on TV wasn't real. But that show made me feel like maybe there was something more in the world, like angels and people who try to do good."

"My kids are still watching those reruns. They get a real charge out of the whole thing—it kind of makes us feel closer, sharing a few laughs and a few corny sentimental moments over that sweet show."

They had done something good, something that connected with people, even if it was on a simplistic entertainment level. Unexpected pride filled Wendie. No matter what happened with the reunion show, this flash of recognition would forever change her perspective on *The Lost Romance Ranch.*

Her eyes automatically sought Teague, who remained almost motionless on the stage, the eye of calm as the hubbub swirled around him.

Teague was special. There was no doubting it. He was a good man who had let his enthusiasm and energy get the better of his judgment sometimes. But at heart he was a kind, loving, decent man who wanted to do the best he could for his family. And the way he did that was by acting. It would be wrong of her to deny him that chance.

"Actually..." She stood. Her knees wobbled. "It's my understanding that the details haven't been worked out. They're waiting for all the cast members to commit before they go forward with work on the script and so on."

Teague looked at her in stunned silence.

The moderator held out his hand to Wendie. "Ladies and gentlemen, I guess you all remember Wendie Keith, who played the rancher's daughter, Claire, in the series."

The gathering swelled with applause and a few cheers.

She dipped her head to acknowledge them, her eyes fixed on her husband. "For the first time since we've been married, I do believe you're speechless," she teased.

"Wendie, what does this mean? What are you trying to say?"

"That I can't expect you to stop making decisions without taking my feelings into account if I don't extend the same consideration to you."

"So, you're going to—"

"What I'm *not* going to do is let you write off any hope that we will do this movie just because I don't like the idea."

He reached one hand out to her, not both hands to ask for an outright hug, just an unassuming gesture of hope and reconciliation.

She took his hand. "Now that I've opened my mouth and stuck my foot in, in front of all these people, would you kindly help get me out of the spotlight?"

"Of course, I will. We're a team, aren't we?"

Her heart soared at the notion even as her mind cautioned against letting emotion run away with her. She and Teague a team again? It was her fondest wish, her most fervent prayer. She only hoped she wasn't setting herself up for disaster.

Ten

Driving on the interstate just doesn't give you the same feeling, does it?" Wendie slumped back in her seat.

"Not really. Do you want me to put the top down?"

"No thanks. Having the top down the whole time got old somewhere on the second day of driving."

"What's the matter? One too many bugs in your teeth?"

"I don't know if it's an age thing or if I've just gotten spoiled." She ran her tongue over her top teeth and winced at the idea of taking a moth in the mouth. "But as long as we're taking the interstate to Albuquerque, I'd rather do it in air-conditioned comfort."

"Can't be an age thing."

"Naw, what was I thinking? Must be all the star treatment we've been getting. It's made me soft."

"You were always soft, Wendie."

She drew her shoulders up, lacing her arms a bit self-consciously over her not-model-slim midsection. "I beg your pardon?"

"In a good way," he hastened to add. "You know, soft and sweet and feminine."

She scowled, trying to decide if that was just a good save or if he meant it.

"It's a compliment, honest. You have soft skin, soft hair...soft lips."

Before she realized she had done it, she placed her fingertips to her lower lip. They had been on the road together four days now, and Teague had behaved like a perfect gentleman. They had laughed, talked, eaten, and worked side by side, and he had never tried to steal so much as a kiss. She had taken that as further evidence that he had changed.

She let her hand drop and sighed. "I must be soft in the head, too, because I'm buying this."

"It's the truth."

"Forgive me if I have a hard time accepting a compliment from a man who bought this in Santa Fe!" She reached into the backseat and pulled a huge black sombrero with silver embroidery and pompoms adorning the brim.

"Hey, hey, hey! That happens to be a lovely souvenir for the kids." He capped the crown of the hat with one hand and plunked it on her head.

"Yeah, I'll bet they fight over who gets to wear it to church next Sunday."

"As well they should."

She leaned over the seat as much as her shoulder strap allowed and rummaged in one of the shopping bags piled in the back. "Along with these!"

A gentle clatter underscored her words as she tugged free three belts, one beaded, one of copper and elastic, and the third of snakeskin with the actual snake's head covering the small buckle.

He played along, laughter in his eyes. "Again, wonderful souvenirs for the twins, as well as pretty snappy fashion statements."

"Fashion statements?" She laced the snakeskin over the rearview mirror so that it dangled down with its blank gaze toward Teague. Then she looped the other belts around her waist and held her arms out. "Saying what? 'Help me, my dad has no taste, and it may be genetic'?"

"I do so have good taste." He frowned, then his expression lightened and he gave her a wink. "I married you, didn't I?"

Her stomach lurched as it would on the sudden downhill lunge of a wild roller coaster ride.

His gaze found hers.

She held her breath. They had talked about life, the endless road, the kids, even the movie deal, but they had not specifically sat down and had "the marriage talk," since he'd pointed out they both had work to do. She'd avoided it, feeling they could not do it justice until the end of the trip. She had not changed her mind about that.

"I mean, think about it, Wendie. I married you, and you, on the other hand, chose me. Now who do you think is the one who ought to be questioning his—or *her*—taste?"

"I had to marry you to keep you from buying things like"—she turned her attention to the shopping bags again—"these."

He feigned intense interest in the long, almost empty highway.

She pulled free a small pair of ornamental Texas longhorns mounted with brass tacks to a red velvet bolster.

"Now, don't start in on those. Those are classy, I tell you, and I know just where I want to put them."

"Yeah, on the front of your car," she teased, plunking them on the dash, where they slid backward until they came to rest wedged between the leather surface and the windshield. "All the gorgeous things you could have picked up in Santa Fe, all those galleries filled with amazing Native American crafts and artwork, and this is what you want to remember your trip by?"

Hands outstretched, wearing the sombrero and two gaudy belts over her "I got my kicks on Route 66" T-shirt, she invited his reaction.

His gaze remained fixed straight ahead as he said, "No, what I would really like to have as a token of this trip..."

She tensed.

"...is a picture of your face if I stop by the side of the road and that family with a flat tire ahead gets a load of that getup and what you've done to the inside of this car."

He would not normally have stopped, not with Wendie in the car. However, they had driven for an hour without seeing much of anyone but huge trucks in a big hurry on the lonely expanse of highway. If he did not stop to offer help, who would?

He swept a wary gaze over the group. A young man wrestled with suitcases in the trunk, obviously trying to get to a spare tire. All the while he kept admonishing the two rowdy red-haired children who ran and screamed in the dry grassy area beside the car.

"They really look like they could use some help," Teague said. "I won't stop if you don't think we should, but I think we should at least see if we can help or offer to call for a tow truck or something."

"I appreciate your asking for my input. My vote is to stop." Wendie had the belts and hat off before their tires eased onto the road's shoulder. When she leaned forward to pry free the longhorns wedged on the dash, she squinted. "You know, I think those people came to the trivia contest and live radio remote we did in Santa Fe yesterday."

He could not place the man's face nor those of the two boisterous children. But they pulled to a stop, and the woman climbed out of the vehicle. He immediately recognized her by her long, dark hair and full, pregnant belly.

"Isn't that the lady who wanted you to sign a pair of wooden angel wings for her baby's nursery?" Wendie slipped the longhorns into the backseat without even looking to see where they landed.

"Yeah, I told her I felt kind of weird about it, the whole angel thing when I'm anything but an angel." He stopped his car and cut off the engine. For a second or two he sat there, giving Wendie time to respond to his remark. He didn't know whether to expect a retort about his most unangelic nature or to hope she would use the opportunity to pay him a compliment. Neither was forthcoming.

"As I recall, she felt pretty strongly about it."

"The lady laughed and told me she knew the difference between make-believe heavenly messengers and the real thing. She just wanted something that seemed more fitting than a slip of paper or glossy photo to remind her of seeing us."

"Of seeing *you*." Wendie waggled her eyebrows to show she was just having fun with him. "I don't believe she asked for my autograph, just spent as much time as she could with you."

"Having that conversation made her really stand out in my mind. I liked her."

"Yeah, but you must not have made a very positive impression on her," Wendie teased. She pointed to the women calling her children to her side, then shepherding them back into the car before shutting herself in as well.

"She's just putting her family's needs first. I can understand that." He gave his wife a pointed look, then opened the car door and slowly got out. "Anything I can do to help you folks?"

"No thanks. I got a spare in here somewhere. Thanks anyway." The man raised the lug wrench in what looked like part-friendly salute, part-implied threat.

Teague stayed standing by the open door of his car. "I have a cell phone. I'd happily make a call if—"

The passenger side of the disabled car flew open. "Oh, oh! Oh, my!"

"What's the matter?" Wendie stretched over the seat toward Teague. "She isn't going into labor, is she?"

"Well, if this were a television show, that's what I'd guess, but—"

"Oh, for heaven's sake!" She lumbered up until her head showed above the blue roof. "It's you!"

The man gave Teague one long, steely-eyed going-over, then his expression eased. "Hey, it *is* you."

"Yes, I'm me, all right, but I never get tired of having that confirmed." He grinned at Wendie. "So now can I do anything to help you out?"

"Thank you, but we couldn't ask—"

"Yes, we most certainly can ask," the husband interrupted his wife's protest. "It's hot, we're on a highway without much hope of getting any other offers, and I have to consider you and the kids."

"That's right." Teague stepped forward.

"But he's a celebrity!"

"I don't mind, really," Teague insisted. "With a second set of hands pitching in, we'll get this taken care of in no time."

The two men worked on changing the tire.

Wendie corralled the young children while their mother rested out of the hot sun. The work went quickly.

"Don't drive on that spare too long; it's just for emergencies," Teague reminded the younger man. "I know it's tempting to skimp and get by when money is short, but you've got to take care of the things that guard your family's safety."

To anyone else it might have sounded like the kind of advice a more life-experienced guy might give to any young family man, but to Wendie the words struck a chord.

"I'll get the tire fixed right away," the man promised.

"Family first." Teague patted the guy on the back.

Mad as she sometimes got about the way her husband could run roughshod over her feelings and focus the best of his energy on his work, Wendie could not deny that Teague had always lived by the very conviction he'd just spoken of. Family first. Whatever he had done, he had done it as his own way of seeing to his family's well-being. She had not agreed with his methods, but she could not now discount his sincerity.

This revelation brought her so much closer to reconciliation with her husband that it made her heart beat faster. The only thing that remained between them, in her view, was the commitment of time from him and her own willingness to let down the walls of apprehension and trust him fully again.

"Don't worry, we're headed straight to the next town to get the bad tire fixed and put back on." The man shook Teague's hand.

The wife motioned to the kids in the car to sit still. She came around to stand by her husband, but her dreamy gaze stayed fixed on Teague. "I don't know how we can ever thank you enough." She dipped her head and gave Wendie a darting glance too. "Both of you."

"We didn't do anything that your everyday good Samaritan wouldn't do." Teague ruffled his fingers through his black hair in his best aw-shucks-'tweren't-nothin' gesture.

"You stopped and you pitched in to help with the tire and the kids." The husband jerked his thumb toward the children in the car. "That sure got things done a lot faster.

On a hot day like today with two little ones and a pregnant wife, that's no small matter."

"You really are like an angel of the Mother Road," the wife murmured.

Teague chuckled. "I'm no angel, but I am a big fan of the One who made the angels. Guess that's why I thought I had to stop."

"Thank you." The man shook Teague's hand again.

The couple turned to walk away.

The wife stole a peek over her shoulder.

Teague and Wendie waved.

The woman bit her lip, then darted back to give Teague a quick kiss on the cheek. "Thanks again."

"It was no big deal, really."

"But it was a big deal to me."

Wendie touched Teague's sleeve, urging him to let the woman have her moment.

"Well, I'm glad I could do something, even a small thing to help someone along the way."

"You have and you did. You see, this isn't the first time I feel like you came to my rescue."

"Oh?"

"I don't talk about this much, but my father was a trucker, and when I was a little girl he'd be gone for long hauls. Seeing your show made me hope that somewhere as he drove along there really was an angel looking over him."

"How sweet," Wendie murmured.

"I prayed for that very thing all the time."

"Then there probably was an angel keeping watch," Teague said. "Just not one like I played on TV."

"I know that now. You see, we never went to church or anything, but when your character started me praying, I began to understand that I needed more than a show to guide me."

"You did?"

"Yes." Her eyes shone. "I started going to church, looking for answers. Then my mom went with me, and pretty soon the whole family became believers."

"God can use anything to lead people to the right way," Wendie said softly. "Even something that just seems like light entertainment, I guess."

"Uh-huh. Your show helped me to find my way, and I wanted to thank you again."

"You're welcome. And I want to thank you for sharing that story with me; it was a real blessing."

The woman nodded then waddled back to her car.

They watched in silence as the family drove off, then Wendie looked at her husband. "Amazing story, huh?"

"Powerful."

"I have to admit, I'm impressed."

"Well, I'm a pretty impressive guy." He winked.

"Oh, brother!" She shook her head at his joking but did not correct him.

"We've done our good deed—what do you say we head on to Albuquerque?" He held out his arms, suggesting nothing more than a sweeping theatrical gesture.

Wendie didn't care why he did it. She walked to him, wrapped one arm around his waist, laid her head on his shoulder, and sighed.

"Something you want to tell me, Wendie?" He curved his hand around her upper arm.

"Nope."

"Something you expect me to say right now, then?"

"Nope."

"Want to just savor the moment of togetherness?"

"Uh-huh." She tipped her chin up and looked at him. "You really are an impressive man, you know that?"

"I...uh..." He blinked. His jaw went a little slack. No snappy comeback came. He just stood there, one arm around her, and looked long and deep into her eyes and smiled.

Finally, she stepped away from him. "We'd better hit the road. We still have a lot of ground to cover."

Eleven

"You know what helping that family with the flat made me want to do?"

Wendie checked the distance to Albuquerque in her guidebook, muttering mindlessly, "Join the auto club?"

"Call the kids."

She jerked her head up. "Ooh, even better."

"It's not much further now. We'll call as soon as we get there. How corny will they think we are for calling just to check in?"

"Well, they are allowed to call home a couple times a week. Since we aren't home for them to call us, we sort of have to call them. Besides I don't really care."

"You don't care about calling them?"

"I don't care if they think it's corny. We're the parents, hon. It's our job to be corny."

"Yeah, but I don't want to embarrass them."

"Are you breathing?"

"Of course."

"Well, if you're doing that in their presence, you can bet you're embarrassing them."

"Me?"

She laughed. "They're almost teenagers now, you know. They have a lock on what's cool, and they know everything in the world. We, however..."

"Wouldn't know cool if we got trapped in a walk-in freezer."

"Just about." She studied his profile a moment, more aware of the silver streaking his temples and of the fine lines fanning out from his eyes and framing his winning smile. "If it's worth anything, I still think you're very cool."

He grinned at her. "Thanks. I think the same about you."

"Aw, thanks. That's not sunburn on my cheeks; you've got me blushing." She put her hands together and batted her eyes, playing up the adoration big-time. "Just think, the coolest boy in the world thinks I'm cool too!"

"Do you suppose that signifies that we're made for each other?"

She swallowed. She wanted to say yes, but if she did, would she be committing herself too soon? This man had hurt her deeply enough that she walked away from him after years of marriage and two children. She had done that despite her belief that marriage was a lifelong promise. Could they really wipe away all the pain, confusion, anger, and disappointment between them in a few days? Based on a few words and superficial actions?

She could not bring herself to suggest as much to Teague. Instead she cocked her head and gave him just the hint of a flirtatious smile. "I suspect it signifies..."

"What?"

She lifted her hands in mock surrender. "That we really *are* as corny as the kids think we are."

~

"And tell your sister to call us as soon as she can. Do you have the number?"

Teague held his hand out to take the receiver from his wife.

"Nine two, that's right. Okay then." She turned her back to him. "Are you sure you have to talk to your dad alone, Sean? I'd hate to think of you keeping secrets—"

"Would you give the kid a break? It's probably about some guy thing," he whispered in her ear.

"Guy thing?" Wendie looked at Teague as if he'd suggested her baby had become an ax murderer.

"You know, he needs money, has his first crush, wants to ask about something he doesn't want to discuss with his mom." He spoke softly, not wanting his son to hear his suppositions. For the first time his son had made the request to speak to Teague alone. That signified a big breakthrough on the part of a kid who had thought his father a big goofball for his part in the breakup of the family. Teague wasn't going to jeopardize that tenuous connection for anything. "Just give me the phone, and I'll deal with it."

Wendie covered the mouthpiece. "First crush? You don't really think..."

"Whatever it is, I'll take care of it. Then I'll give you the full report, if it's not divulging anything said in confidence. Okay?"

She hesitated.

He held out his hand. "Then when Kate comes back from her horseback ride, you can have a private talk with her, to even things up."

"This isn't a contest."

"Mom? Mom, are you still there?" Even Teague could hear his son's voice coming through the receiver.

"Um, yes, sweetheart. I...uh, I'm glad you're having such a terrific time, and it was wonderful to talk to you. I'm going to give the phone to your dad now and go out and get a soda, so I won't even be in the room to hear whatever it is you think you have to—"

"Wendie, this call is costing us a bundle." Teague slipped the phone from her hand. "Your mom says good-bye and sends her love, Son."

She bit her lip.

He waved his hand to shoo her out of the room.

"Tell him to brush his teeth and be sure to put his dirty clothes in the plastic bag I packed for him."

"Your mom says to brush your clothes and put your teeth in a plastic bag."

She scowled.

"Yes, apparently she *has* had too much desert sun. But she's going to remedy that now by going and getting a nice cool soft drink." He gave her a nudge.

Her scowl deepened, but she started toward the door.

He waved again.

She sighed. "All right. I'm going. But I'm trusting you. Whatever this is, you will take into account my feelings on the matter?"

But I'm trusting you. The words went straight to his heart. "You can count on it."

She gave one curt nod, then slipped out the door.

"Okay, Sean, what's so important that you wanted to talk to me alone without your mom in the room?" Teague leaned back against the headboard and kicked his legs up on the bed.

"I...um..."

"Out with it, Son. What's the big mystery? You run through all your money already buying sodas and bubble gum from the canteen?"

"I don't like bubble gum."

"What then? There's a girl in your group you think is cute, and you want to know how to get her attention?"

"No." Utter annoyance came across the line in the one syllable. "Nothing childish like that, Dad."

Did he feel put in his place. "Then what's so important that we had to keep it secret from your mom?"

"Yesterday, a real-estate agent, and not the lady Mom worked with about this place, either, just stuck a big sign up on the property."

He suspected he knew the answer before he asked it, but remembering that he was dealing with a twelve-year-old, he had to ask anyway. "What kind of sign?"

"It says 'Commercial Property for Sale.' "

He sat up. "Really?"

"Yeah, and the thing is, they asked me and another boy to help put the sign up, so I got to hear all about it."

"And why would you need to tell me this in private, without your mother here to listen? She's the one who has her heart set on buying that ranch." Though he had to admit that more than a time or two the prospect of settling down in this part of the country had intrigued him, too. "Why don't you want to tell all this to her?"

"Because, Dad, while we put the sign up, the camp owner and the real-estate lady talked about how much money they wanted to buy the place."

"They did?"

"And I know how much Mom said she could afford to pay."

"Really? I know you said Mom talked to you and your sister about finances so you wouldn't worry, but you're saying she told you what she could pay for the ranch?"

"She told the real-estate lady the price range she wanted to look for with us standing right there, Dad."

"I see."

"And let me tell you, the price she had the real-estate agent looking for and the price they said they could get for this place are nowhere near the same range."

"*Nowhere* near?"

"If their price was in Texas, what Mom could afford to pay would be somewhere in California."

"That's pretty far apart," he said softly, touched by the double meaning behind the choices his son had made. "Too far."

"Now you know why I didn't want Mom to know, but why I had to tell somebody."

Somebody? The word cut through him. He wanted to be more than just *somebody* in his son's life, in the lives of his entire family.

"I had to tell you, Dad. Because I thought you'd know what to do."

"You did?"

"Sure. You may have been gone a lot of the time..."

That hurt.

"...and busy with work when you were around."

So Wendie wasn't the only one who had felt that way.

"But I never doubted you'd always come through for us."

That helped. Somewhere, deep down, his son trusted him. He could breathe easier knowing that he had not totally alienated his children as he had his wife.

"Even when Mom moved us to Texas, I thought you'd figure out a way to fix things. That's why you came out and took Mom on this trip, right? To try to fix things?"

"It's what I hoped for. What I'm praying will happen."

"Then can't you find some way to fix this, too?"

But I'm trusting you. Wendie's words came back to him again.

"Mom had a lot of big dreams about owning that ranch and living there."

Suddenly Teague thought he saw a way to prove to Wendie once and for all he had changed his workaholic ways. In one selfless action he could save his marriage and restore his family. It had no small appeal that in doing so he could literally save the ranch, too. "Tell me, Sean, can you get me the phone number of the real-estate office handling the sale of that place?"

Wendie opened the door and, once she saw that Teague was off the phone with Sean, let herself back into the room.

Teague remained vague about what her son had wanted, telling her they'd talk about it later. Then he announced he had something to take care of and would return soon.

Wendie welcomed the quiet time in her room. She had so much to think about and so much left to decide. The time spent in her husband's company drew her toward the conclusion that he had honestly changed. She felt real hope that given time and work they could become a family again. Unless...

The issue of the reunion movie loomed in her thoughts. It divided her heart even more now than it had before she started the trip. On one hand, meeting the fans and hearing about the show's effect on people made her long to recapture that time for them, and even for herself and Teague.

Still, the haunting words *what if* echoed in her mind. What if doing the show just plunged Teague back into his old ways? What if the show was a tremendous success, and suddenly other offers began to pour in? How could she expect him to turn his back on those, and if he did, would he forever hold it against her? What if the show was a laughingstock? Would it crush her husband's spirit beyond repair or make him feel he had to work even harder to prove his critics wrong?

The many scenarios troubled her. She got up from the bed to get a drink and caught a glimpse of herself in the mirror. Her dark blond hair shimmered with golden highlights and platinum streaks from riding in the convertible in the southwestern sun. Though she had used sunscreen, her skin bore a robust glow. She had lost the pasty pallor she'd noticed when she began the journey. Her eyes shone clear, and she no longer wore the weariness of the past three months like a shroud around her shoulders.

She looked healthy, confident, and at peace with God and her life. She looked...like Claire, or the way she imagined the character would have looked all these years later. Well, almost.

She grabbed up her hairbrush from the counter and whisked it through her hair, made a center part, then started making sections. In matter of moments she sported the trademark hairstyle of her character, twin braids pulled straight back from the hairline, lying neatly against her head and hanging down to brush her back. It took years off her face, though she suspected she could thank the pull of the tight braids for most of that. Still, it lifted her spirits to see it, like meeting an old friend who had been on her mind and out of her life far too long.

She cocked her head at the image in the mirror. Would it really be so bad to do the show? To let go of her need to control everything and trust her husband fully once again?

The jangle of the telephone cut through her thoughts.

"Hello?"

"How much longer on your tour, Mom?"

"What's the matter, honey? Are you okay? Is Sean all right?"

"I'm fine. Sean's fine. I just have to know when you'll get back to the ranch."

Wendie gripped the phone receiver more tightly as

she asked, "We'll be there to pick you up Saturday, just as we planned. Why?"

"Because I have some bad news."

"What?"

"They've put the ranch up for sale."

"That sounds like good news to me. Great news, terrific news!"

"You don't understand, Mom. They just put it up for sale this afternoon, and they already have a bidder for it."

"You're kidding." Wendie's throat went dry.

"The real-estate agent and the owner kept gabbing on and on about it right in front of me as I waited my turn to use the phone."

She sank to the bed. "I don't suppose they mentioned how much the buyer offered for it?"

"Not as much as they wanted to ask for it in the listing, they said."

"That means there's still a chance I can top the bid." Wendie started to tuck her hair behind her ear, then remembered her braids. "Did they...did they mention any actual prices?"

The number Kate gave made Wendie's head spin. "I don't have it."

"But you could get it, right?"

Wendie went over her financials as best she could with her heart pounding and a cold sweat working its way up from under her collar. "Maybe if I..."

If you buy that ranch in Texas, you will have done it mostly with money I earned acting. She thought of the warning Teague had given her early on in the trip. And of her response... *If I do this reunion show, that money could go toward my buying the ranch.*

She looked up and stared at the reflection in the mirror. "I could get it. I'd have to make some quick calls and do some fast talking, but I really do believe that I can get it."

Twelve

"You know, when I thought about coming on this trip, I figured we'd just see small towns and roadside attraction type places all the way." Wendie raised her face into the dry air whipping past them.

"We've seen our share of those."

"True. And then we saw Albuquerque."

"Impressed?"

"Very. Not at all what I expected to find on this quasi search to find the remnants of Route 66. In fact, the idea of cities never really clicked with whatever vague notions I had of the old road."

"Well, the cities anchored the route and kept it thriving." Teague steered the car with one arm straight, the other elbow crooked over the door of the open convertible. "Makes more sense when you know it wasn't built as one long stretch of highway. It was pieced together by connecting existing roads."

"Quite a unique part of the American experience, isn't it?" She scanned the horizon, her heart filled with the beauty of the mesas and the constant changes in the landscape.

Even though they'd gotten away later than planned,

they'd slowed their pace today. They wanted to enjoy the remarkable scenery and to travel over as much of the original route as they could. That meant some creative maneuvering and vigilance with the signs and road map. It was worth the effort.

"But it's also sad." Wendie pulled her hair into a ponytail to keep the wind from thrashing it about too much. As she wound the elastic band around a second and third time, she squinted behind her dark glasses.

"What's sad?"

"That so much of something that shaped our country was just abandoned, left to decay."

"It's sad whenever people decide to throw away something good rather than fighting to preserve it."

She tensed.

"No metaphor for anything personal intended," he added, and in doing so made her even more aware of the twin applications of his statement.

She pressed her lips together and looked away. "It must have been something in its day, don't you think?"

"The road?"

"Uh-huh. Bright lights and big cities, open spaces and freedom accented with every kind of crazy tourist trap imaginable."

"And the natural beauty. The landscape is still breathtaking along so much of the way."

"One day maybe we could join one of those restoration groups and take the whole trip—Chicago to L.A."

Teague glanced at her. "I'd like that. Very much."

She wrapped her arms around herself. During the whole trip she hadn't spoken in terms of the two of them making future plans. Now, thinking of the energy she'd poured into making private plans to protect her dreams should things not work out with her husband, she felt awkward and embarrassed. "How far are we now from the Continental Divide?"

"Not far. You want to stop? Could make another fine photo opportunity."

She checked her watch, calculating the time differences between there and Texas, between there and California. "No, just passing over it is enough for me. What about you?"

"We had such a late start getting away from Albuquerque today. If we putter around too much, it will be dark by the time we pull into Gallup. Not that I mind. All the neon and flashing signs—driving up on those just after dusk might be a scene to remember."

"Is that a yes or a no?"

"That's a..." His mouth quirked up at one side. "That's a 'whatever works for you,' darling."

"Then I say no. Let's push on and forget the photo op. Besides, that name, Continental Divide, doesn't sound like the kind of thing I want to write under a picture of the two of us."

"Can I take that as an encouraging sign?"

"What do you think?" She tipped her head to one side and smiled. She hoped that came off as cool and elusive instead of betraying her anxious feelings.

"Then let's head on to Gallup. Have to admit, I'm really looking forward to that stop."

"Because of its notoriety as a place of wicked indulgence?" She held up her guidebook. "Says here it once had a quite a reputation for recklessness and wild times."

"Too bad they've worked so hard to rehabilitate the town's image. We'll have to behave ourselves."

"I don't know." She stole a sidelong glance. "Even when you behave yourself, you can be a pretty dangerous guy."

"Is that why you avoided me so much the past couple days?"

"Avoided you?" She forced out a laugh, buoyant yet unconvincing. "When have I avoided you?"

"Ever since the twins' phone calls. If I didn't know better, I'd suspect you have some kind of hidden agenda all of a sudden."

"Well, you haven't exactly been Mr. Forthcoming yourself. I seem to recall catching you a few times murmuring into your cell phone, your eyes all shifty like a B-movie private eye."

"You know me, always working on a deal."

"So maybe you're not the only one."

"Oh?"

She'd said too much. She had her reasons for not letting Teague in on the early stages of her plan, and she wasn't ready to discuss it with him yet.

"Is there something you want to tell me, Wendie?"

"No."

"No?"

She angled her shoulders in his direction. "Is there something you want to tell *me?*"

He opened his mouth. His chest rose with a deep breath. He shut his mouth, narrowed his eyes, and shook his head.

She wished that hadn't piqued her curiosity so much because she could not pursue it without calling further attention to her own cache of secrets.

He braced his arms straight, but his eyes peered over the top of his sunglasses to catch her gaze.

She clutched her guidebook to her chest. "I've changed my mind."

"About telling me something?"

"About stopping at the Continental Divide."

"Why? You decide you *would* like those words under a picture of us?"

"No." She put her hand on his arm. "Not at all. I just need a little space."

"Space?"

"To stretch. Move around." She shifted in the seat. "Besides, it's the Continental Divide."

"So you said."

"The stony ridge that creates the natural division between east and west," she read from her guidebook.

"And dividing me from the subject we were on. You said something about not being the only one making deals?"

"Water falling west of this line flows to the Pacific Ocean, and east of it, to the Atlantic." She held the book up as if totally absorbed in the writing. "It's the highest point on Route 66."

"And yet a definite low point in the conversation for me."

"It's 7,275 feet above sea level."

"No chance of drowning my sorrows then."

"You don't have any sorrows."

"Maybe some curio shop there sells them. They have just about everything else."

"Oh, that reminds me, there's something here on the businesses located on the Divide and how they got—"

"Wendie!"

"What?"

"You win. No more questions about deals and avoidance. Of course, you know this means we have to actually make a stopover at the Continental Divide."

"I said I wanted to, didn't I?"

"So you did. You got your wish. We're stopping. But when we do?"

"Yes?"

"I'm confiscating that guidebook."

"Smile!" Wendie pressed the button on the small black camera as its owner directed. It whirred, then sent off several rapid flickers of light. Finally a brilliant flash sparked brighter than the others in the impending dusk.

"Just one more, please, Mr. Blackwell? In case that one doesn't turn out?" The woman in pink shorts, red shirt, and orange baseball cap held her two squirming children in place before her.

Teague agreed.

Wendie got off a great shot.

The woman thanked them both. She hesitated before saying good-bye outright. But when her children ran off screaming about which one got to sit where in the minivan, she took off after them.

Wendie went and stood beside Teague. She sighed as they watched the last of a small cluster of fans depart. "I cannot believe you."

"Me? What did I do?"

"Here we are at the geographical backbone of the continent. Dead center in the middle of the middle of nowhere. And you get recognized by no less than a dozen people."

"One person." He held up his finger as he slipped one arm around her shoulders and propelled her back toward the convertible. "One person recognized me, asked for an autograph, then showed it to someone else. After that it just sort of snowballed."

"That's what I mean."

"What?"

"Only you could have something snowball in the middle of a desert in summer!"

He laughed. "So a few people besides you still think I'm kind of cool."

"And you love it." She jabbed him in the side.

"Not as much as you might think." He stopped and turned toward her.

With the daylight fading quickly and the chill of the night air gathering around them, it felt good to stand so close to him. It warmed her. It gave her the sense of safety from whatever lay outside the circle of his arms, of confidence in whatever lay ahead of them.

"You don't love it?" she asked.

"Not as much as I love you." He swept his hand back over her hair. "You do know that however I may have acted in the past, whatever I may do that falls short or fails in your eyes, I do love you with all my heart."

Tears filled her eyes and clung to her lashes. She blinked and they rolled onto her cheek. Cooled by the breeze almost as soon as they fell, they stung on her hot skin. She swallowed but could not clear her throat enough to speak. So she simply nodded.

"Do you believe that?" he pressed on.

"Yes." She lifted her chin. "Yes, I do."

"And you trust me again? I don't know how we can ever hope to build a life together if you don't fully trust me to put my love for you first."

"I trust your love." She made a point of not saying she trusted his motives and actions. She did, but her own guilt over her secretive schemes of the last few days made it hard for her to speak about the subject. "Teague, I..."

"Let's not talk it to death, Wendie. You said you trust me. That's what I needed to hear."

The next instant his mouth settled over hers, and he pulled her close.

She wound her arms around him, letting her fingers sink into the thick, coarse hair at the nape of his neck, and gave herself over to the moment. Only then did she realize how much she had missed her husband—and that if they wanted this to work out for real, she had to tell him everything.

He broke away, murmured her name, then kissed her again.

Lost in his embrace and her own dizzying emotions, she promised herself she'd tell him later, when both their heads had cleared.

Gallup sparkled on the horizon like a tangle of gaudy costume jewelry against a dark cloth. Tourists had flocked to this place since the twenties. It had reinvented itself from a rowdy railroad town, to a second home for the Hollywood glamour set, to the "Indian Capital of the United States," a center for Native American arts and crafts. The demise of the Mother Road had not killed Gallup, which had had its bleak times, to be sure. It had survived, cluttered with glowing signs and the ghosts of times past.

The sight stirred Teague's imagination and added a touch of nostalgia to his thoughts. "Route 66 runs through the very heart of Gallup, you know. Just look at the lights and advertisements. I loved the scenery we took in today, but this…this is the kind of imagery I think of when I picture the heyday of this old road."

"It does look like something from an old postcard, doesn't it? There's something so familiar about it."

"Maybe because it's been a favorite movie locale."

"Really?"

"Oh sure, and the El Rancho here"—he pulled the car into the lot of a large hotel-motel complex—"used to be a favorite place for movie stars to stay."

"Then they should be ready for us." She patted her ponytail as if it were some fancy bouffant hairdo worthy of an old-time celebrity. "Do you think we should wear our sunglasses when we go in, even though it's dark outside? You know, to keep up the mystique?"

"The only thing that will keep up is your insurance

rates, when you start bumping into things and falling down stairs."

"That might have a mystique all its own."

"You're sure in a silly mood tonight," he said as he parked the car.

"Whimsical," she corrected. "Hard not to be in a city with so much neon and kitsch flashing at you from everywhere."

"This place is great, isn't it?" He looked up at the hotel.

"It's all been great. Really, the whole thing has just been..." Her voice trailed off. She sighed.

"Yeah, its been memorable, to say the least. But I've looked forward to seeing this hotel in particular the whole trip."

"Really? Why this one?"

"Oh...the history, the renovation, the...history."

"You said that twice."

"It has more than one history. It began as one thing, went through some bad times, and now has changed for the better."

"That's a history I can relate to."

"Wendie—"

"Hmm?"

"Let's make a pact now just to relax and enjoy our evening here. No talk about movies or deals or anything like that, promise?"

"I...um..."

He put his finger to her lips. "Promise?"

"Okay."

"Terrific."

It had been a cheap ploy to buy time so he could finalize the ranch deal. But it had also been the truth.

He had looked forward to the famous El Rancho ever since he'd seen the ranch Wendie wanted to buy. Now that he was on the verge of making that a reality for her, he couldn't wait to see the completely restored hotel and motel. The business he and Wendie would run would be nowhere near as flashy, but this fine old landmark could serve as worthy inspiration.

He'd have to be discreet as he studied the décor and setup. He'd settle for buying postcards of the place rather than trying to scope out all the ingenious embellishments and commit them to memory. He'd make excuses to go down hallways and talk to guests. Since he and Wendie would have separate rooms, he'd sneak out late tonight and talk to the staff and learn as much as he could in a short time.

He took Wendie's luggage out of the trunk and handed her the smallest case. For a moment he thought of blurting it all out to her—his decisions, his plans, his bid to buy her the ranch of her dreams—but at the last second he held back.

News had come of someone else interested in the property, someone willing to top his offer. If he told Wendie about buying the ranch now and it fell through, he'd feel rotten. More important, for Wendie to get her hopes up about her dream ranch, then to have the place bought out from under them, would simply break her heart.

Teague looked down into the eyes of his beloved wife, eyes that now looked again on him with trust that he would take care of her and the family. His breath caught in his chest. In that instant he vowed he would do anything to keep from hurting her again. That meant he would have to keep his secret just a little while longer.

Thirteen

"Where do we stand on the revisions for the reunion show?" Wendie held the telephone receiver close to her ear, although no one was in the room to overhear even her side of the conversation.

"You're not a big enough star to demand final approval of a movie script." Her old friend, Haley Preston, an entertainment lawyer working to find out what she could about the movie deal, spoke with calming efficiency. "You don't have creative control handed to you; it's the kind of perk you have to earn. You do understand that, don't you, Wendie?"

"Of course. However, I'm the final holdout from the original cast." She tried to pace as she talked, but the phone cord restricted her movements. "They have to sign me or no deal, right?"

"No deal on *this* project."

"*This* project?" She sank to the bed. "There are others?"

"There are always other projects."

"But this is a reunion of a very specific show and cast."

"You haven't been away from this town so long you've forgotten that someone is always pitching a new idea or working on the next hot treatment."

Wendie sighed. Loudly.

"My take is they could be swayed to do something else entirely with the reunion show if it looks like this version won't pan out."

"Like what? A musical revue? A retrospective? A cartoon special? I can't even fathom what else they could do."

"I've stopped trying to second-guess what they might or might not try to put on TV."

"Scary, huh? But point taken."

"And at any given moment they could scrap the project completely, leaving you without anything if you don't move to a contract stage soon."

"A contract." She turned away from the morning light streaming in through the curtain windows. "That's such a big step."

"Well, you'll have to sign a contract."

"I know, I know. It's just that..."

"Listen, I only know that you need money and they are ready to talk money."

"They are?" Wendie's pulse picked up.

"I think so."

She thought back over the phone call she'd made just moments ago to the real-estate agent. They still stood a chance of buying the ranch, but they'd have to sweeten the offer to better that of the first bidder. "Do we know how much money yet?"

"Nothing in writing, but in the ballpark of what you say you need."

She wished the producers would either come through with heaps more money than she needed or else turn her down cold. That would have made everything so much easier. This hurry-up-and-wait, back-and-forth was what gave her headaches and made her doubt her every move. "I guess being in the ballpark is better than striking out."

"Sure, but if you put yourself on the life's-too-short list by making a lot of creative demands they don't think you're worth..."

"The life's-too-short list?"

"Life is too short to put up with her nonsense."

"Oh." That kind of list Wendie understood.

"Think about it. If they can revise the script to suit you, they can also revise it to delete you."

"So what do you think I should do?"

"Hard truth?"

"I can take it."

"I think you should talk it over with your husband."

Wendie drew in her breath and wound the phone cord around one finger.

"I know, I know. You don't want him to get his hopes up that you might do this movie when you'll only commit to it if you must in order to buy that ranch. Though why anyone would want a ranch in the middle of nowhere is beyond me."

"It's not in the middle of nowhere—it's in the middle of what's left of Route 66." That mattered to her now, though it never entered her thoughts before. "It's a place where I can work with horses, give lessons, and hold camps, even special ones for people with special needs. And the twins love it there."

"What about Teague?"

"Well, when I first looked into the ranch, the whole

idea was to give me a new home, identity, and business without him. The ranch was my independence."

"Wendie, I—"

"Now...well, it's not that so much has changed. I still see the ranch as my venture. It's my dream. Whatever happens between Teague and me, I don't want to give it up."

"When I asked about Teague, I—"

"I just don't know if he's the ranch type. I can't imagine him walking away from the business to muck stalls and check in hotel guests. Or I couldn't before taking this trip with him."

"Actually—"

"He swears now it's the work that drives him, not the fame, you know?"

"I—"

"If that's true, there's plenty of work on the ranch to occupy him. He'd be *with* us as well as working to take care of us. That way he'd be providing for his family in every way, not just financially."

"Wendie! I'm not asking 'what about Teague living on this crazy ranch?' I meant what about talking this over with him?"

"Oh. I should. I want to. When I think we're both... ready."

"He's the best one to get advice from on the movie, and he's the only one who can tell you if he wants to live on a ranch or not. Why don't you just sit down over a big breakfast this morning and—"

"I can't. He's at a local TV station doing one of those sunrise shows, then he's going to shoot some promos for reruns of *The Lost Romance Ranch* that the station is airing this fall." She glanced at the clock on the bedside table. "He expects me to have breakfast and be ready to roll as soon as he gets back midmorning."

"Then talk in the car."

"It's a convertible. Really hard to have any kind of serious discussion with the wind whipping around us like that." She put her hand over her eyes and winced at the transparency of her excuses. "I should hang up and get busy. I still have to pack and eat."

"Okay."

Wendie coiled the cord around her finger.

"You're not hanging up," Haley said.

"I just...I don't know what to say to him, Haley. How to approach this."

"Just do it."

"It's not that easy. I'm in a King Solomon situation."

"A what?"

"No obvious way to win. Looks to me that I have two choices, and neither is guaranteed to solve my real problem."

"Tell me the two choices, and I'll see if I can help."

"Well, I can do the movie and buy the ranch. Then I risk losing him forever because he won't make a home there."

"Or?"

"I don't do the movie, I don't get the ranch, and he can't forgive me for costing both of us our dreams with my stubborn, uncooperative actions." That wrapped up her hesitancy like a TV program guide summed up a ten-hour miniseries in two sentences. "So that's it. Where's King Solomon when you need him?"

"You can figure this out, Wendie. You and Teague can figure it out together."

"Maybe."

"If I had to choose, I'd do the movie and try to buy the ranch, working on both with the man I love."

Wendie's breath caught in her chest. "I like the idea of doing a reunion, especially now that I've met so many fans of the show and heard their stories. I'd love to do something wonderful to thank them, but that script is a turkey."

"Giving thanks, a turkey—maybe you can do a holiday show instead."

"Wow, do you think we could find someone to produce that kind of thing?"

"I think you're asking the wrong person. Talk to your husband, Wendie."

"I will." She said good-bye, then hung up the phone and whispered, "Probably."

"Are these the postcards of El Rancho?" Small talk, a pretty sorry stalling technique. Still, she picked up the paper bag lying on the seat between them. "You've sure got a lot of them."

His shoulders twitched. "I told you, I like the place."

She shuffled through them. "These are kind of fun to look at though. I can see the appeal. I wish we'd gotten postcards of all the places we've been on this trip."

"We have plenty of pictures."

"Yes, but the postcards sort of bring the whole Route 66 imagery together. And they show the places in different ways. Like this one." She held up a postcard of the El Rancho lobby decked out for Christmas.

He stole a glance at it but said nothing.

"Doesn't this just make you want to come here for the holidays?"

"Never was one for spending the holidays away from home."

She ducked her head, painfully aware of the deeper meaning in that remark. "Well, if this was your home, or rather, if your home was something like this...you know, southwestern, ranchstyle, wooden beams, stone hearth, open range for miles."

"Open range? At El Rancho? The place sits in Gallup right on old 66!"

Her subtle nudges toward extolling life on a ranch had no effect. "Grumpy this morning, aren't you?"

"Just tired."

"Because you had to get up at five to make it to that sunrise show?"

"And I didn't get to bed until very late last night."

"Oh?"

"Couldn't sleep." He shrugged. "So I poked around the hotel, talked to the staff. That kind of thing."

"Oh." She had nothing to add to that. She certainly couldn't start doling out true confessions and seeking his input on her decisions, not with him in this mood.

The conversation became as sparse as the landscape. They reached Arizona and traveled on in silence. After a series of tiny towns they met with a gravel road and a dead end. It did not improve Teague's surly disposition to have to turn around and go back to the interstate.

"The scenery takes your breath away, doesn't it?"

"Mmm."

"Looks like something described in a western novel, huh?"

"Uh-huh."

They stopped at the Petrified Forest National Park and Painted Desert and took a few pictures.

"I wonder if, when we got these photos back, we'll be able to tell which are the petrified logs and which one is you!" Wendie teased when they got back to the car.

"Right now I'd rather be sawing logs than seeing them," he answered.

"Then why don't you let me drive so you can rest awhile?"

So she found herself behind the steering wheel, rolling across some of the most beautiful stretches of the country while Teague snored in the seat beside her. Not much chance for meaningful dialogue there.

"Don't suppose you'd mind if we zip off old exit 286 and see the Wigwam Village Motel in Holbrook?"

His head drooped to one side. His mouth hung open.

She took that as a "go right ahead" and guided the sleek car toward the landmark, a Route 66 favorite.

The semicircle of concrete teepees, stark white against the brilliant blue of the Arizona sky, made the perfect backdrop for a photo of Teague, fast asleep in the red convertible.

He snoozed as they passed the string of black-and-yellow signs advertising the Jack Rabbit Trading Post and as they then passed the store itself.

Wendie didn't mind as much as she thought she

might. She found herself lost in the atmosphere of the drive, in the nuances of the high desert. She went on through Winslow, reluctant to disturb her husband's rest, and skipped a stop in Meteor City, a tourist attraction centered around a crater.

Halfway between Winslow and Flagstaff, their final destination on the tour before they headed back to get the kids at the ranch, she spotted Two Guns. Route 66 was gone here, but the ruins of this old attraction still stood. Rusting gas pumps stood vigilant over the crumbling buildings that had once housed mountain lions, or so the words worked in stone above the doors promised.

Her heart heavy, she thought of the ranch she longed to buy, the 66 Central Guest Ranch and Grill, later named the Flying C, and its connection to the Mother Road. She wondered if it might someday end up like Two Guns and so many of the other unique places that had once thrived on "America's Main Street" unless someone like her took it over.

She couldn't let that happen. But she risked letting it happen if she didn't act soon, and to make the right decision she had to talk it out with Teague. As she turned the car toward Flagstaff, she made up her mind. She would confront her husband about all this today.

A harried young man met them at the entrance to the bookstore in Flagstaff and introduced himself as Jason. Teague introduced Wendie to him, then took her arm as Jason rushed them toward the designated area where a small crowd formed a semicircle around a long table. David Penn was already seated behind a pile of books. He waved a greeting when he saw them push through the group.

"I can't believe you guys really showed up." Jason swept out his arm for them to go ahead of him. "This is phenomenal. Ryder and Claire here! No one thought we could pull it off, and then when you were ten minutes late—well, my manager started saying you weren't coming."

"We just got a little turned around." Teague pulled out a chair for Wendie, then leaned in to whisper, "and around and around."

"Watch it."

"I'd rather watch you."

"Why? Are you afraid I'll lose my sense of direction and take a few spins around the table before I notice we're right where we wanted to be all along?"

He chuckled at her reference to her attempt to find the store by the directions given over the phone. "Actually, I just like looking at you."

Jason gave him a pat on the back. "If you would, just a say a few things about yourselves and your connection to the book."

"Thanks, Jason, I appreciate your work on this and apologize for being late." Teague pushed Wendie's chair in, then sat down next to her.

"That was nice." Wendie nodded to the young man her husband had just spoken to so encouragingly and went on in a low voice. "You know, in a lot of ways, you've shown more patience and generosity to me and even to total strangers on this trip than I've shown with you in a...in a long time."

He wanted to ask her to elaborate in hopes she'd finally say the three little words he'd wanted to hear this whole trip.

"You go first."

"What?" Teague looked up to find Jason standing at his shoulder.

"The author has already said a few things about himself, and now if you would—not that I would ever tell you how to do things."

Teague looked at his wife, his chest tight but his mind open to the young man's suggestion. He'd told his wife he loved her, yet he'd kept so much from her. Maybe before he deserved to hear her confess her love for him again, he needed to tell her everything. "In truth, it's not a bad idea, Jason. Maybe I will go first."

"Then go." Wendie pointed toward the murmuring group.

"Hmm? Oh, okay."

A flash went off as someone snapped a picture.

"Hi. I'm Teague Blackwell, and I want to say a few words to you today about real life."

"This should be interesting," Wendie said out of the corner of her mouth.

"I know you came first and foremost to buy David's terrific book." He held a hand out toward his friend.

A surge of applause suitable to the quiet atmosphere of a golf match rose briefly from the group.

"But many of you came or have wandered over from the other side of the store because you remember Wendie and me from our days on television."

A larger smattering of applause answered.

Wendie beamed a smile at that, which took him by surprise. She actually appeared open, relaxed, and upbeat about the reference to the show and characters she had left behind so long ago.

"Television is not real life." Teague continued with his planned speech, but his gaze kept darting back to Wendie's contented expression. "Television is how we think we want real life to be. Or is it? Would you honestly want to live your life on the back roads of Route 66, without a real home, without a long-term goal other than to get the next job, do the work for all you're worth, then move on again?"

If the audience had ever seen or heard of *The Lost Romance Ranch,* they would identify that speech with Teague's portrayal of Ryder. One look in Wendie's eyes confirmed that she knew he spoke of the man behind the character.

"That's exactly how I've lived my life, folks. And it hasn't been easy."

"It hasn't been all bad either," she whispered.

"Everywhere I go, the character Ryder is always right there with me. Sometimes he's even standing right in front of me so that the person I'm talking to isn't talking to me at all, but to him."

Teague surveyed the intent faces of his audience and let his words pour straight from his heart.

"Sometimes the edges between my real life and my television life blur together, and I find myself believing that I'm somebody special. But I'm not. I'm just a guy, maybe with a little talent, who's worked hard and found himself blessed with a role that spoke to people's hearts."

Wendie inched her chair close to him.

He sensed she wanted to take his hand or say something to him, but he continued talking. "In real life I'm the proud father of twins, and I'm married to a wonderful, understanding woman. I wouldn't trade that for the best script in television history."

The crowd applauded. But Teague's gaze focused on Wendie, whose eyes glistened with impending tears. He ran his hand up the tight muscles of his neck.

"Real life," he began again, "is love and family and a lot of the good stuff."

Wendie slipped her hand in his, gave it a squeeze, then let go.

"But real life is also mortgage payments and unemployment—something I know a little bit about—and working your behind off just to keep up with the cost of groceries. It's high crime and traffic jams and worrying about the kind of world our children and grandchildren will grow up in."

Teague paused for effect.

"So in the end, if real life gets to be a little too much, and dropping in on Ryder and Claire on *The Lost Romance Ranch* gives you a break from your troubles for a while, then I'm glad we could be a part of your life."

The audience broke into warm, enthusiastic applause. Television affected people. He, in his small role in it, had affected them. He didn't need a reunion show to prove that to anyone, most of all himself.

He sat down.

Wendie seized his arm. "That sounded perilously close to a good-bye speech!"

You go first. The words echoed in his head. He had to tell her about the ranch. "Wendie, I..."

"Ms. Keith?" Jason motioned to Wendie, then toward the crowd.

Wendie touched his cheek, then stood.

"I'd like to echo everything my husband has said today, especially the bit about being glad to have been part of a cherished memory for so many people.

"I've met quite a few fans of the show this last week. I've also gotten to know a lot more about Route 66, the subject of David's book and the setting for *The Lost Romance Ranch.* Both have touched me in ways I had not imagined they would."

Teague watched the faces of the crowd as they listened to her. In the few moments after she had finished speaking and they began signing books, he decided, that's when he'd talk to her.

"And I've realized I want to keep my connection to the old road and to that show alive."

If ever he'd heard a cue for a major announcement, that was it.

"That's why I'm happy to make it known today that I am going to agree to make the reunion movie of *The Lost Romance Ranch.*"

"What?" He shot out of his chair.

She turned to him, her face beaming. "I'm going to do the movie! Aren't you thrilled?"

She threw her arms around him, and he stiffened. "Stunned is more like it. Why the big decision all of a sudden?"

"That's the best part about it."

He braced himself to hear just about anything at all.

"I'm doing the movie to get enough money to buy the ranch of my dreams!"

Anything, he amended, but that. "Are you kidding?"

"I've never been more serious. Why?"

"Because you can't buy that ranch."

"Why not?"

"Because I already bought it!"

Fourteen

Wendie's fingers ached from holding the pen in a death grip during the two-hour signing. Her cheeks ached from keeping her best all-is-well-with-the-world smile in place. Her whole body ached from the tension coiling through her muscles. But most of all her heart ached from the realization that nothing had changed this last week, least of all her husband.

They drove in silence to the place where they would spend the night before making the ten-hour trip via the interstate back home the next day. Wendie waited in the car while Teague registered them. Minutes later he got in the car and handed her a plastic key card.

"They didn't have adjoining rooms available. We're in 129 and 131." He drove them around to park in front of the red doors with brass numbers on them. "We've got a couple from Little Rock between us."

"I can live with that."

"Sure that's far enough apart for you?" He gave her an impish grin, his green eyes baiting her to lighten her mood. "I could see if they have something on an upper floor. Might help us rise above all this."

She glared at him, jerked open the car door, and got out.

"Get it, upper floor? Rise above?"

She clenched her jaw and let the door fall shut with a *wham*.

"What?" His door slammed shut harder than hers had, making the car jostle as he came around to the back. "What have I done to make you this mad, Wendie? Other than make it possible for you to have the home of your dreams?"

She grabbed her overnight bag from the open trunk without a word and headed for room 131.

The trunk banged shut behind her, but she didn't look back. From the corner of her eye she saw him reach his door just as she stopped in front of hers.

"I don't get this, Wendie." He tossed his leather travel bag to the ground and faced her. "I thought you'd be happy. I thought you'd—"

She stuck her plastic key card into the slot. Her eyes fixed on the tiny red and green lights that were supposed to tell her when the door could open.

"Fine. If that's the way you want to be. Don't talk to me about it." A soft *ka-chunka* told her he'd unlocked his door.

The handle on Wendie's door did not budge.

Leather scraped concrete, followed by a muted thud. She peeked to see that he had nudged his bag into the open doorway with the toe of his boot. Any second he would walk inside. Even though it was scarcely five o'clock, if she didn't say something right now, she knew she probably wouldn't see her husband again until morning.

His door creaked as he pushed it open.

She yanked her key out. "I thought you had changed!"

"I beg your pardon?" He stepped toward her. "Are you speaking to me now?"

"I don't know why I bother, since you never listen." She shoved the card in and waited for the green light.

"Never listen? That's all I've done since we began this trip."

"Oh yeah? Then why did you rush ahead with your own plans without considering how it affected me and the kids?" She pulled the card free and groaned in frustration.

"Here, let me." He took the card from her hand, slid it in, then back out again. The green light flickered. He turned the handle, and the door swung open on a dark, musty-smelling room.

She pressed her lips together.

He handed her the card. "I *did* listen, Wendie. You said you wanted that ranch, and I did everything in my power to get it for you."

"Get it for me?" She held the door open with her arm straight. "I didn't ask you to get it for me."

He chuckled. "Well, at the price they wanted, you couldn't get it for yourself."

He was right. That indisputable fact only fueled her anger. She flicked on the light switch and pitched her overnight case onto the bed.

"What is the big deal, Wendie? I took your needs into account and put them first, just like you demanded."

"Excuse me? Demanded? I *demanded?*"

"Yeah, I think when someone puts a requirement on

a relationship that says 'my way or the highway,' even if she couches it in very mature terms, it's a demand."

"My way or the—"

"Maybe you don't recall that you left me. Took my children and moved off to another state. You wouldn't even discuss the situation with me until I promised I would show you how I had changed."

She tipped her chin up and drew in a deep breath.

"And you had cause."

She exhaled in a stunned whoosh.

"I will grant you that. Being around the kids those few days without the distractions of my work, being with you this week, having so much time to think things through, I will admit it. You had cause."

She blinked, and to her surprise, tears dampened her lashes.

"Cause to demand more of me as a husband and father. And I have tried to give you that. I thought by buying the ranch I'd make it clear to you that I'm willing to give you all of me, my time, my attention, and all my love."

A hard lump rose high in her throat.

"But now it seems even that isn't good enough."

"It's keeping it a secret from me, charging ahead with your own plans without talking to me, that hurts so much." She sniffled. "Why didn't you just tell me about it?"

"I could ask you the same question."

She could not look him in the eye.

"This whole trip, the one thing I wanted more than anything to gain from you, the one thing that I thought we had to have if we hoped to rebuild our marriage, was trust. I wanted you to rediscover your trust in me."

"I know. And I have."

"Then why did you keep *your* plans a secret from me?"

"You did know I wanted to buy the ranch and that I was thinking about whether to do the movie." She tucked her hair behind her ear and studied the toes of her shoes. "You buying the ranch on the sly, that came out of left field."

"No, that came out of my love for you and the kids." He turned and walked the few steps to his room. He pushed his bag, which had been propping the door open, inside. Then he looked up. "I'm sorry if you can't see that. Good night."

His door fell shut.

She stepped toward the sound.

Her door fell shut.

She sighed, stared at the plastic card in her hand, and began to cry.

I'm sorry if you can't see that. Good night.

He should have stopped after the first two words. Teague dropped to the bed and buried his face in his hands. Exhaustion, confusion, and anguish all welled up inside him, but he still had the presence of mind to understand that he had been wrong. Wrong in his actions, if not in his motivation.

He'd listened. He'd put the family's welfare first. He'd provided for their future. And he'd done it behind his wife's back. He had deserved her trust, but he had not *acted* worthy of it.

Of course, she hadn't exactly provided updates on her own activities either. He straightened his shoulders, his defenses rising. The problems between the two of them were not one-sided.

He got up from the bed, walked to the window, and pushed aside the dark, heavy curtain. The late afternoon sun hit the sleek lines of his red car. The chrome gleamed. The glare of the light hitting the windshield stung his eyes. He and Wendie had come so far in that convertible, in miles and in their relationship with each other. They had not talked about it incessantly, but as two people married fifteen years, they had not needed to, the way young, insecure lovers might. They had started to mend their marriage on this trip through laughter and shared experiences, just focusing on being together.

Images of the last week filled his mind. Getting caught in the rain, taking photos at all the Route 66 landmarks, meeting their fans, helping that family stranded by the roadside.

You really are like an angel of the Mother Road.

Teague recalled what the woman had said to him that day—and his reply to her: *I'm no angel, but I am a big fan of the One who made the angels.*

That's what was missing in the whole equation. They had tried to work out the problems in their marriage without taking things to the One who made that marriage matter.

He let the curtain fall shut, closed his eyes, and

offered a short, sincere prayer. Now he would go to Wendie and see if he couldn't help her see where they had both gone wrong.

~

She had only done what she had to protect their fragile relationship. Somehow the prideful justification gave her little comfort. She had been every bit as sneaky and secretive as he had been. Only for her it had been worse. She'd laid down the law about what she expected of him, then proceeded to break that law coming and going. That they both believed they'd made the right choices for each other's sake did not make it right.

But what would she do differently?

"It's a King Solomon situation." She rummaged through her overnight case, not really looking for anything in particular. She wasn't usually given to fits of talking to herself, but since she was seven hundred miles from anyone else likely to listen to her ravings, she went on. "A King Solomon situation without the solution. If only I had the same resources as—"

She sank to the bed. The movement made her overnight case tip forward. Her toothbrush and cosmetics and all the odds and ends inside clattered and spilled onto the bedspread. Wendie ignored them.

It was so simple. Why hadn't she thought of it before? She did have the same resources as Solomon, but neither she nor Teague had shown the wisdom to turn to that resource.

She leapt up and ran to the door. She had to tell

Teague this. She had to apologize for her behavior, then make him see what she had just realized.

"Wendie? Open up. It's me."

"Teague," she whispered. Her hand hovered over the door handle. For a fleeting second she wondered if he was still angry. Then she realized it did not matter. What she had to say would heal the hurt and heated feelings between them as water soothes the parched earth. She opened the door, ready to speak first.

He beat her to it. "We're a couple of first-class idiots."

"I couldn't have said it better myself."

"What were we thinking?"

"Thinking? You call that thinking?"

"Yeah, too much thinking, when what we really needed to be doing was—"

"Taking this to God," she finished for him.

"Exactly." He put his hand on her cheek. "*And* talking it over with each other."

"No argument here."

"I think those are the words we should put up over the ranch door." He held his hands out as if framing the words on a plaque. "No argument here."

She laughed. "You know, the reason I didn't tell you about trying to buy the ranch was—"

The jangle of the telephone cut her off.

"Who'd be calling you here?" Teague followed her inside.

She shrugged and shook her head as she snatched up the receiver. "Hello?"

"Mom?"

"Kate?" The camp had a list of every hotel and bookstore on their itinerary in case of emergency, so she didn't waste time asking how her daughter had gotten the number. "Honey, what's wrong?"

He hurried to her side. "It's Kate? Is she all right? Is Sean all right?"

Wendie held up her hand to quiet him so she could hear.

"Mom, there are two things I have to tell you."

"The first thing you have to tell me is that you and your brother are okay."

"We're fine."

"They're fine," Wendie relayed to Teague.

He mouthed a thank-you to heaven.

"At least, we're fine now."

"Now?" She wondered how she'd made any sound with her heart pounding in her throat. "What do you mean 'now'?"

"Well, we're okay, better than okay, just great for now, but...we're a little worried about how we'll be when you and Dad get here and find out what we've done."

"What have you done?" She reached out to take her husband's hand.

"We, that is, Sean thought it up."

Wendie heard her son's defiant "You went along with it" in the background.

"Thought *what* up?"

"The plan."

"The plan?"

"The plan?" Teague echoed as he leaned in close to hear his daughter's side of the conversation.

Wendie almost did not want to know. But she was the

mom. Her job description required that she ask, "What plan?"

It all began to spill out. The reason for the private phone calls, the information fed separately to each parent about the sale of the ranch, the hope that somehow this would be the thing to make their family whole again.

"Mom, we just figured it would make you and Dad have to work together. But when we heard the tour guide—"

"Betty Jo?" Wendie thought she remembered the woman's name correctly.

"Betty Jo Byerly," Teague added with a grin that said not only did he remember the lady, he found this convoluted mess the kids had made quite funny.

"Yes, Betty Jo Byerly. When we heard her giving a tour yesterday to some people passing through, and she said the ranch had two offers and was in a bidding war between two people with Hollywood connections..."

"Your well-intentioned little plan kind of blew up in your faces, didn't it?"

"Like parents, like twins." Teague winked at her.

Wendie sighed. He had a point. "Okay, honey. I'm glad you came clean about this before we got there. Your father and I will deal with all this when we pick you up the day after tomorrow."

"What are you going to do about the ranch? Is Dad still going to buy it? Is he going to move out there and us stay in our apartment?"

Wendie put her hand to her forehead. "We'll talk about that Saturday, honey. That's the best I can tell you right now, except that your dad and I love you, and no matter what happens with the ranch, we're all going to be all right."

Teague glanced down, then met Wendie's gaze without hesitation. "I didn't tell you about the ranch because I knew that you couldn't afford it and that there was another bidder."

"Hello?" Wendie, leaning back against the headboard, held up her hand. "Me!"

"But I didn't know that." He laughed, and sprawled out as he was, the whole bed shook. "I had all kinds of fears that some big Texas rancher in a ten-gallon hat was ready to best my highest bid without dipping any deeper than his pocket change."

"I don't know about a ten-gallon hat, but I do know where I can borrow a real tacky black sombrero."

"Smile when you say that, partner."

"Partner." The word came out like sigh. And she did smile.

He got up and went around to kneel beside her. "I kept my secret because I was afraid I'd lose the ranch."

"And I kept mine because I was afraid I'd *get* the ranch." Her expression softened from teasing to tender as she added, "And that would mean I'd lose you."

"Never going to happen." He touched her face.

"I believe you." She ran her fingers back through his hair.

He sealed his promise with a long, sweet kiss.

Saturday morning they drove up to the Flying C with a renewed sense of purpose, for their marriage, their family, and their future. The twins were there to greet them, looking excited but anxious.

Wendie leapt from the car first and started to run toward her children, thrilled with all the good news she had to share. Just a few feet away from them, however, she remembered the unwritten law of parenting adolescents: *Don't do anything to embarrass me.*

She pulled up and settled for a quick kiss on the cheek for each child and a light squeeze.

Teague did not respect the unwritten law, however. He wrapped his daughter up in a big hug.

Kate giggled and returned the affection in kind.

When the man held his arms open to his son, Sean stepped backward.

"C'mere, I just want to give you a hug, Son."

"I'm not coming over there until I know just how mad you are at me over the real-estate deal."

"Aw, nonsense." Teague went to the boy. "What? Are you afraid I might accidentally let my hands slip and turn a sincere welcome home hug to...this?"

He pretended to slide his hands to the boy's neck.

Kate laughed.

"Not with everyone watching, Teague." Wendie stepped up as if to intervene, then whispered, "Wait till we're home and we can really make him pay."

Sean waved his hand to dismiss the kidding. "Yeah, right, like you guys would ever beat me or hurt me."

"No, but I have a list of chores a mile long..."

"Only a mile?" Teague stroked his chin. "Then maybe we should postpone the punishment for his coming up with this harebrained prank until after."

"After?" The boy looked from his father to his mother. "After what?"

"After we move to this ranch."

"We're moving?" Kate squealed.

"You bought it? You bought the Flying C?"

"We're not going to keep that name, but yes, looks like we'll be full-time Texas residents from now on." Teague opened his arms to encircle both children.

"Dad, when you say 'we,' do you mean...?"

"All of us. The whole family." Wendie stepped up and put her hands on her children's backs to complete the circle.

"But what about Dad's work?" Sean's expression grew serious.

"There'll be plenty for me to do on this place."

"And actors don't have to live in California anymore. If there's a job he really wants to do, it's just a short hop on a plane." Wendie smiled at her husband.

Sean screwed his face up. "While you guys were gone, did you learn to be ventriloquists? Because I swear the right words just came out of the wrong mouths."

Teague laughed.

Wendie joined him. "No, we're not throwing our voices. It's no trick. What we did learn on this trip, however, was the art of listening, of taking one another's needs into account before we make decisions, and of trusting each other again."

"And of never forgetting we're not angels, but we are loved by the One who made them." Teague pulled the family into a big, warm hug.

At that moment Wendie knew they were truly home.

Epilogue

Two weeks before Christmas that same year

"Wendie, this was a brilliant idea." Teague laced his arm around her shoulders. "Just brilliant."

She swept her gaze over the chaotic crush of people moving in and around the ranch lobby. Men in jeans and sweatshirts adjusted mammoth lights. A boom mike hung overhead. Two television cameras stood at the ready just beyond an area marked off with masking tape.

"I can't take all the credit. I got the idea from you and Haley."

"This isn't going to be another King Solomon connection, is it?"

"No." She jabbed him lightly in the side. "Haley first mentioned to me that the reunion of the show's cast did not have to be in movie form, and she jokingly suggested we do a holiday show. So when the movie deal began to fall apart..."

"Okay, I can see that. But where did I come in the picture?"

"Not in the picture, hon, in the postcard."

"Huh?"

"The postcards you picked up at El Rancho? Remember how I admired the one of the lobby at Christmas?"

He nodded, his green eyes filled with unmistakable pride and joy. "And now look what's come from all that."

She did look. She couldn't help it. It all still amazed her to think she'd actually convinced a television producer to shoot a Christmas special with the cast of the old show right from her family's new home.

The front room of the old 66 Central–Flying C Ranch positively glittered. Thick evergreen boughs laced with silver tinsel rope hung over the stone fireplace. Fat red candles glowed from polished brass bases twined with holly, and tiny lights twinkled from every corner. Even the set of longhorns Teague had brought home from their trip and tacked above the doorway sported a sprig of mistletoe.

"You did a great job getting all this organized, Wendie."

"I had a lot of help."

"Georgia and Jett pulled out all the stops to make sure the food was perfect, despite how busy they've been with the new baby." She waved to the owners of another nearby Route 66 establishment, the Double Heart Diner.

The tall man with silver hair raised his hand in greeting. His pretty wife, with a deep green elf hat perched at an angle on top of her I-Love-Lucy red hair, lifted her three-month-old son's chubby hand to wave too.

"And Starla Mae Jenkins went to great lengths to get her brother, Elvis, away from law school long enough to sing us a few carols."

"Why do I think she didn't have to work too hard to get him to do that?"

Wendie grinned at the brother and sister, who both

looked like they'd just stepped out of another era, then at her husband. "You put in your fair share of work too. Hauling in that ten-foot tree was no small effort."

He twisted around. The blinking lights from the tree at their back splashed colors on his cream sweater. "When I saw how many ornaments we collected from Route 66 enthusiasts, well, we had to have a big tree to hold them all."

Wendie tilted her head back to see the top of the tree and the unusual angel that graced it. "I have to ask you. Why did you pick the angel from the mayor of Cupid's Corner for the topper? Is it because she worked so hard on helping us come up with that Route 66 wedding and honeymoon package?"

"Which has already gotten us six reservations, thank you." He gave a thumbs-up.

Wendie scanned the people milling about the lobby until she spotted Jenny and Joe Avery talking with Betty Jo Byerly, who still gave daily tours of their newly renovated guest ranch. "Or is it because the mayor and her husband came down to take part in this celebration with us?"

"It's because I like that angel. She reminds me of you."

"I thought you were the angel of Route 66."

"Places, everyone, places." The call rang out over the quiet.

"Do you know where you're supposed to be, Mr. Retired-from-Acting-but-Might-Be-Lured-Back-for-a-Great-Role?"

"Hey, that's Mr. Retired-from-Acting-but-Might-Be-Lured-Back-for-a-Great-Role-If-It-Doesn't-Interfere-with-His-Family-Life, if you don't mind."

"I don't mind. Not one bit." She rose on tiptoe and gave her husband a quick kiss.

"Places," the voice called out again.

"Well?" Wendie raised her eyebrows.

"I know my place." He gave her a wink. "It's anywhere that you are."

"And mine is wherever you are." She gave his hand a squeeze, then motioned to the twins to join them by the tree.

Last-minute instructions went out for the final dress rehearsal. The room fell silent, and Wendie's heart filled with pure joy in the season and in the promise of all the seasons to come as Teague went through his opening lines.

"I'd like to welcome you all this evening to our show and to our home. It's because of this place that Wendie and I rediscovered the things that matter most to us—our family, our faith, and our love and commitment for one another. So it only seemed fitting, given our history, both public and personal, that we have named our little ranch, just off what was once Route 66, something that will remind us of the time we almost lost it all. Ladies and gentlemen, Merry Christmas from *The Lost Romance Ranch.*"

If you enjoyed Annie Jones's
Lost Romance Ranch,
ask for *Cupid's Corner* at
your local bookstore.
The following is an excerpt
from *Cupid's Corner*.

If wedding plans have got you draggin'—

Costs arisin', in-laws naggin'—

Pack your bags, don't be a dope—

Grab your bride and just elope—

If she hollers, give her a kiss—

And cart her off to wedded bliss—

Hurry now, you're on your way—

To Hitchin' City USA!

Cupid's Corner, Kansas
The Elopement Capital of Route 66

—road signs enticing couples to take their vows in Cupid's Corner circa 1951

Introduction

Welcome to Cupid's Corner, Kansas, a town that exists only in this writer's fanciful imagination but typifies the romance, nostalgia, and whimsy so often attached to the real towns and attractions that once did and still do populate Route 66, the Mother Road.

While you will see some references to real places found on the old road, this place and the characters who populate it are fiction. It is my goal to allow the fantasy setting and characters to enhance and complement the real people and places found on the few miles of Route 66 that jog across the southeast corner of Kansas. There is, to my knowledge, no town holding a record for the most marriages between the Fourth of July and Labor Day, no special laws regarding marriage licenses in any one Kansas city. (I did my research and found that certain cities and counties in other states do have the right to issue immediate marriage licenses, while the rest of the state must adhere to that state's regulations regarding waiting periods.) Still, the possibility that such a place with such a history could exist sure does add a spark of fun to the proceedings, doesn't it?

I hope you enjoy your visit here in my little invented corner of Route 66 and that you come back often to visit and read book one in the Route 66 series, *The Double Heart Diner.* These are all fictitious places too, at least until you read the stories and get to know the characters. Then, I hope, you may feel they are "real" in your imagination and populated by old friends who are finding their happily-ever-afters somewhere along the remnants of old Route 66.

You are cordially invited
to the wedding of
Jennifer Kaye Fox
and
Alex Stephen Michaels
at Cupid's Corner Methodist Church
Two o'clock in the afternoon
The second of July...

Prologue

June 25

"Here comes the bride, all dressed in..."

"Never mind what I'm dressed in!" Jenny Fox held up her hand. The long ribbons of crisp white bathroom tissue intricately wound around her entire body in a simulated wedding gown rustled as she shook with quiet laughter. Streamers of the cheapest grade of coarse paper, fashioned into a veil and clamped to her head with half a dozen bobby pins, trembled around her shoulders. "Would somebody just take the picture so I can get out of this getup? The games are over. Let's get on to the good stuff!"

"And those, my friends, are the very first words our bride will say to her husband after saying 'I do.'" Jenny's sister, Bobbie Ann Fox-Mayfield, waved one hand in the air with a flourish to signal that the games at the bridal shower had concluded. "Punch and cake in the dining room, everybody! Then Jenny can open her gifts and realize what good taste we all have despite the fact that we've all grown up and live in what the groom-to-be considers a one-horse town without the horse."

Jenny winced to hear again her fiancé's running joke about the small town of Cupid's Corner, Kansas. Alex Michaels had been born here, just as she had. He'd grown up in a cottage house one street over from the two-story colonial she was now standing in, the very house the two of them would soon occupy as husband and wife after they bought it from her parents.

Jenny wrapped her arms around her chest, crushing the hastily draped paper that looped around her neck and encircled her waist. Try as she could to picture herself and Alex Michaels living in this house, the image simply would not come into focus for her. Celebrating holidays, raising a family, having Sunday dinners after church, growing old together here—none of the things she associated with her future in Cupid's Corner came clearly to mind. That scared her a little. A bride—even one in a tacky paper dress—should have those kinds of warm, wonderful thoughts, shouldn't she?

Jenny chewed at her lower lip and tried to push down the anxiety rising in her chest. Pre-wedding jitters. That's what her mother had called it when Jenny had tried to tell her she was having second thoughts. Not that she didn't love Alex—she did—but she just couldn't help but wonder how two people with such different hopes and dreams could be happy together forever, especially if it meant one of them would have to give up those dreams.

Alex had always spoken of wanting out of the small-town lifestyle, of moving away to try the excitement of a big city. Jenny struggled to convince herself every day that this phase of his life had passed—that his years away at college and then med school had satisfied that restless longing to live elsewhere, and that he was ready to settle down.

She'd certainly had her fill of life outside the haven of her hometown when she'd gone away to finish her education. After graduating from Kansas State University two years ago, she couldn't wait to get back to the people, the places, the values she held so dear. And she'd brought with her a renewed enthusiasm to preserve everything that made this town special. She would use that enthusiasm and more at her new job working for the chamber of commerce.

Who was she kidding? She pretty much *was* the chamber of commerce. It had taken her two years of letter writing and campaigning, but she'd finally convinced the town council to hire someone to head the chamber on a paid basis, allowing that person to give the task their all. And Jenny was that person. It was not a responsibility she took lightly. The floundering town's prosperity might now well rest on her ability to represent and market the town well.

She smiled to herself and twirled one strand of long, curly dark hair around her finger, biting her lip to still the flutter of anticipation in her stomach. At last, she could give back to Cupid's Corner some of what it had given her.

"Look at her, lost in a daydream. I bet I can guess about what...or should I say about who? Or is it whom?" Jenny's mother put one hand on Bobbie Ann's back to nudge her toward Jenny.

"Oh, we all know what she's thinking about." Bobbie Ann moved to stand next to her sister. "About the day she wears her real gown and becomes Mrs. Alex Michaels."

Jenny sputtered something unintelligible and let it go. How did you explain to the women who had done so much to put together a huge wedding that you were more focused on your new job than your new husband?

Jenny's mom didn't give her the chance to explain anything anyway, as she gestured broadly, waved a disposable camera in the air, and cried out, "Now, big smiles, girls. Think about those gorgeous, successful men of yours and say 'diamonds and emeralds and rubies'!"

Bobbie Ann gritted her teeth and obliged. "Diamonds and emeralds and rubies."

"Oh my!" Jenny tossed in.

"Jenny!" Mom clucked her tongue as she lowered the brightly colored camera from her eye. "How can I take a picture if you're going to clown around like that?"

"Mom, I'm dressed in a—" She broke off, looked at Bobbie Ann, and sighed with good humor. "Oh, never mind."

Their mom did not get her reputation for being ditsy without cause. Still, she was a good woman and one terrific mom, and Jenny knew the joke about the jewels had been just that, a joke. Mom had never encouraged them to seek material wealth in a mate but to marry for love—hopefully to upstanding, churchgoing men.

Alex was both, or at least he had been. Though his schedule had affected his church attendance these last few years, Jenny assured herself that he'd get back into the routine again after their marriage. She felt the Lord must surely understand about doctors missing church services, especially when they worked so hard to help as many people as possible, as Alex would soon be doing.

As a doctor, Alex could play a big role in sustaining the independence and viability of their community. With some not-so-subtle nudging by Jenny, Alex had admitted he could serve his residency under old Doc Hobbs at what had once been the county hospital but was now really more of an all-purpose clinic and emergency-care facility. That situation would suit Alex perfectly since he had specialized in emergency medicine, and Jenny believed it would give Alex a chance to get reacquainted with the slower pace of life here. Then eventually he could take over the clinic for the older doctor, who had been his mentor and, even more, like a grandfather to Alex.

It all seemed so perfect, perfect for Doc, perfect for the town, perfect for...well, everyone. Didn't it? Jenny clenched her fist, wadding bits of her "gown" into her damp palm.

"Now, stand together, girls, and smile."

Just the sound of her mother's sweet voice assuaged the tension building in Jenny. Jenny wondered what she was worried about. Once Alex returned to live in Cupid's Corner in two weeks—after their wedding next week and the honeymoon to end all honeymoons—he would love the life here as much as she did. This town that Jenny cherished, that held her hopes for the future as well as her fondest memories of the past, would become their home forever.

A blinding flash startled her out of her reverie.

"Isn't that just precious?" Jenny's mom raised the tiny camera like a spokesmodel, so that Jenny wasn't sure if her sometimes flighty mother meant to compliment the picture, the paper gown, or the product. "Now stand still, girls. Bobbie Ann, move in closer to your little sister, and for goodness' sake, smile! I want to take another photo in case the first one doesn't turn out. This is a picture Daddy and I will want to take with us to Arizona."

The mention of her parents' impending departure from Cupid's Corner struck a sad chord in Jenny's heart, but she knew that her father's health, which had been poor for nearly two decades, demanded the change. Both he and her mother would have a better quality of life in their retirement condo, while Jenny remained here, intent on improving the quality of life for everyone in this town.

"Smile, Jenny. Smile. This is a landmark occasion, you know. My two girls, one about to be a bride, the other about to be a mommy for the first time!"

"Mom!" Bobbie Ann's face went beet red.

"Oh! I wasn't supposed to tell yet, was I? Well, surprise!" The flash went off to underscore Mom's words despite the fact that she had the camera pointed at the carpet.

"No kidding, surprise!" Jenny's heart leapt with sheer joy at the news her mother had gushed out, obviously without Bobbie Ann's consent. She turned to her sister, suspecting her eyes might just bug right out of her head as she asked, "Is that true? You're...you're..."

"Yes." Bobbie Ann's face radiated happiness from her sparkling green eyes to her high, round cheeks and easy smile.

Everyone said the two girls looked like twins in their faces but like two strangers in their builds, as Jenny was long-limbed and lean while Bobbie Ann was a few inches shorter and nicely padded, as Bobbie Ann's husband,

Mark, liked to say. Nicely padded and about to get more so, Jenny suddenly realized.

She threw her arms around her sister for a big hug, and as their mother's camera flashed again, Jenny whispered, "When did you find out? How far along are you? Why didn't you tell me?"

"I didn't want to detract any from your big celebration, so I've kept it a secret for a few weeks. I planned to make the announcement after the wedding." Tears bathed Bobbie Ann's eyes, and she sniffled.

Jenny felt her own emotions begin to swell. She reached up and tore off a length of the white paper still adorning her head and body and handed it to Bobbie Ann. "I know you two have been praying about having a baby for a long time now."

"Yes, we have. And I think more than half the town has been praying right along with us." Bobbie Ann dabbed the tissue at the dampness on her cheek.

"That's one reason I love this place so much—people are willing to do whatever they can for others." Jenny blew her nose on a scrap of what had been her pretend wedding gown. "All these years that Daddy has been sick, they always did so much to help us out."

"Speaking of helping out, I'm going to have to count on you more than ever now, with Mom and Daddy leaving. And Mark's promotion to regional manager means he'll travel a lot, and—"

"Say no more." She took Bobbie Ann's hand. "I'll be here for you. And for the baby. I'm not going anywhere, I promise."

This time Bobbie Ann yanked free a strip of tissue to

blot her eyes. "Thank you so much, Jenny. I knew I could depend on you. Everyone always knows they can depend on you, Jenny. That's why the town placed its trust in you with that new job. You won't let them, or me, down for anything."

A hard lump filled Jenny's chest at that tall order, but she did not let her expression show any doubt or concern. The two of them simply stood there for a moment, crying softly and pulling off pieces of the tissue bridal ensemble as the need arose.

"Now, no tears, you two. This is the happiest time of our lives, you know." Mom gave them each a hug and planted pink lipstick-smeared kisses on their cheeks. Then she straightened away, holding up the camera. "Got to get some pictures of the cake before Aunt Maddie demolishes it trying to cut out the piece with the most sugar roses on it."

Bobbie Ann and Jenny both laughed.

Mom hurried off.

Jenny began to follow when Bobbie Ann caught her by the hand and pulled her back. "She's right, you know. This is the happiest time of our lives, so far. Just like we used to dream. Our lives are turning out perfectly in every way."

"Yeah, perfectly." For one heartbeat, Jenny thought of hugging her sister tight and pouring out all her doubts and reservations. But Bobbie Ann's condition and the promise Jenny had just made to always be the one her sister could rely on stopped her cold. She managed a smile, cleared her throat to chase away any lingering weakness in her voice, and said, "Everything is going to be all right for both of us, Bobbie Ann. Everything is going to be perfect."

"Jenny, are you sure you're all right? You look a little—I don't know—worried, unsure. Are you having second thoughts?"

Jenny bit her lip to keep from suddenly unburdening her reservations on her pregnant sister. Jenny loved Alex and trusted in God to make their union strong; that was enough to make it all work out, wasn't it? It had to be enough. She opened her mouth to reassure Bobbie Ann that all was well when the doorbell cut her off.

"Who could that be?" Bobbie Ann's tone rang with quiet irritation at the interruption. "Everyone we know is already here."

"Probably a delivery." Jenny pounced on the opportunity to get away, clear her thoughts, and put herself back in a better frame of mind. She gave a carefree smile. "We've been getting them all week from Alex's med-school friends."

"Ooh, then you'd better go see what it is." Bobbie Ann must have bought Jenny's relaxed act, because she gave her sister a hug and joked, "Coming from the doctor type, it could be something good."

"Ha! These folks aren't getting doctors' salaries yet. More than likely it's something they got a discount on through the school. One of them actually tried to pass off a petri dish as an ashtray."

"What doctor would give you an ashtray?"

"One that couldn't think of any better disguise for a petri dish, of course." Jenny headed toward the door, seizing the chance to get away from the party and pull herself together.

She strode purposefully down the hallway, her dress swishing around her ankles as it began to sag and droop in the places where she and Bobbie Ann had helped themselves to bits and pieces. Jenny thought about pulling the whole thing off before she opened the door, but with the veil pinned on tighter than an old maid clinging to the bridal bouquet, she decided against it. Explaining the big picture—the shower, the game, the photo—seemed infinitely easier than trying to relate to a total stranger why she had toilet paper bobby-pinned to her head, she quickly decided.

The bell rang again.

"I'm coming, I'm coming, hold your horses, would—" She swung open the door to find Alex on her doorstep. Her heart leapt, not from wild, romantic love, but from the clash of emotions created by her anxiety over the marriage and her fiancé's sudden appearance.

"How can I hold my horses, Jen? This is strictly a one-horse town, you know, without the—"

"One horse," she filled in for him without missing a beat. She blinked to let her eyes adjust to the bright summer sunlight that seemed to turn Alex's sandy hair to a lustrous gold and bounced off the glaring white of his shirt as it stretched over his broad shoulders.

"Nice dress. Did you get it off the rack or off the roll?" His mouth lifted into the kind of smile that usually made Jenny's knees wobble.

This time her entire body reacted, tensing and stiffening as though bracing to take a blow.

"Why are you here, Alex?" she said so softly it hardly stirred the wisp of tissue that lay against her cheek. Had he come to tell her he'd been suffering the same confusion she now felt? Did he also wonder if they could really make their vows last a lifetime despite their many differences? She wanted to know, but then again, she did not want to know. She wet her lips. "You weren't supposed to get into town for two more days. What's wrong?"

"Why does something have to be wrong? Couldn't I just have wanted to see the prettiest girl to ever wear a designer wedding gown by Charmin?" He crooked his finger beneath her chin. "Nothing is wrong, Jenny. In fact, things could not be more right. I have some exciting news to tell you, and it just couldn't wait another minute because it's going to mean some big changes."

"Changes?" she murmured. She did not like the sound of that. A cold sense of dread gripped deep in the pit of her stomach. The one thing she had hung her hopes on, the one thing she had let herself believe would ultimately allow it all to work out was that things would go exactly according to her plans. *No changes*. "Alex, what are telling me?"

"I applied to do my residency at one of the best hospitals in Kansas City—"

"You never told me. When did you do that?"

"Awhile back, before we got engaged." He dashed it off as if it excused his hiding from her this piece of life-altering information. "When I applied doesn't matter anyway, Jenny; it's when they want me to start that's so exciting. Next week. Can I come in so we can talk about this? We've got a lot of things to deal with and not much time if we hope to be moving to Kansas City right after the wedding."

"No." The word sounded as quietly stunned as she felt.

"No, what? No, I can't come in? I saw all the cars out there and remembered it was your shower, but since I'd come all the way to the corner of nowhere I—"

"No." She said it this time with more conviction.

"No? No to what? Jenny, you're not making any sense!"

"No, you can't come in. No, you can't just change everything like this. No, we cannot move to Kansas City right after the wedding. No. No. No."

He clenched his jaw. "Jenny, be reasonable."

"No," she whispered. "You kept this a secret from me, led me to believe that you were content with my plans for us when all along..." She had to swallow hard to choke back the bitterness rising in her throat. The reality of what was happening began to sink in, and a dull ache began to throb in her heart. Her world was falling apart on her own doorstep while she stood and watched in a toilet-paper wedding dress. It almost made her want to laugh out loud. Almost.

Instead she asked Alex Michaels to leave, told him that she would see to the details of calling off the wedding. He tried to protest but not too hard.

Moments later, when he climbed into his shiny new sports car, he turned and called back to her, "Jenny, are you absolutely sure this is something you won't regret later?"

All she could do was lift her hand to wave good-bye to send him on his way and whisper to herself the answer to his question: "No."

ASK FOR THESE OTHER BOOKS
IN OUR ROMANTIC COMEDY LINE
AT YOUR LOCAL BOOKSTORE!

Suzy Pizzuti
Halo Hattie's Boarding House Series:
Only God could take hard-of-hearing Halo Hattie's fervent prayers for the wrong things and make them right!

#1 Say Uncle...and Aunt: Sean Flannigan and Julia Evans, two high-powered executives, are suddenly on baby-care duty and unexpectedly fall for more than the baby.

#2 Raising Cain...and His Sisters: Olivia Harmon is struggling to heal after a tragic loss. Only the arrival of Cain and his sisters can bring her out of her shell again!

Shari MacDonald
The Salinger Sisters Series:
Meet four sisters, each of whom has her own escapades while falling in love.

#1 Love on the Run: Cat Salinger wants one thing: the big new ad account. However, her chief competition (and major distraction in the love department), Jonas Riley, proves to be more than Cat bargained for.

#2 A Match Made in Heaven: Lucy Salinger is a fantastic matchmaker. But will she find the cute new doctor a wife—or keep him for herself?

#3 The Perfect Wife: After her husband divorces her, Felicia begins a new life. But her new male housekeeper cares for her more than she dreams!

Barbara Jean Hicks
The Once Upon a Dream Series:
Classic fairy tales, retold in modern times—with a comic twist!

#1 An Unlikely Prince: A professor rents a quiet cottage in a distant town to accomplish his writing goals. Little does he know that his lovely neighbor is running a day-care center for seven imps straight out of Snow White!

#2 All That Glitters: Cindy Reilly launches a hilarious self-improvement campaign to win the heart of her chosen prince. Thanks to an eccentric "fairy godmother" and a disagreeably snooty stepmother, her campaign works—but not the way she'd planned!

#3 Loves Me, Loves Me Not: A beautiful woman is through with romance—until a mysterious pen pal unexpectedly trips up her heart. Then she discovers her sweet, sensitive mystery man is her miserable, undependable, utterly beastly ex-husband—and he wants her back!

Annie Jones
The Route 66 Series:
Meet some incredible characters along historic Route 66—who'll steal more than your heart!

#1 The Double Heart Diner: Georgia Darling's mission seemed simple: Save the Double Heart Diner. But things have become more complicated since sophisticated Jett entered the picture. She likes him, maybe too much, but it's clear she can't trust him. Can she save the diner—and her own heart—before it's too late?

#2 Cupid's Corner: The feisty lady mayor of a small Kansas city on a stretch of forgotten Route 66 is trying to reestablish its title of Hitchin' City USA by staging a summer wed-a-thon. Will the mayor and the editor of the local newspaper find themselves with their own irresistible itch to get hitched?

#3 Lost Romance Ranch: Built by a brokenhearted cowpoke years ago, the once famous dude ranch is now the subject of legal wrangling. When a separated couple is sent off on a treasure hunt along Route 66 to see who will win ownership of the land, can they find the love they've lost along the way?